TEXAS
HORSETRADING CO.

Also by Gene Shelton
in Large Print:

Tascosa Gun

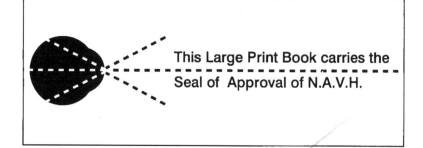

TEXAS

HORSETRADING CO.

GENE SHELTON

G.K. Hall & Co.
Thorndike, Maine

Published in 1998 by arrangement with The Berkley Publishing Group, a member of Penguin Putnam Inc.

G.K. Hall Large Print Western Series.

The text of this Large Print edition is unabridged.
Other aspects of the book may vary from the original edition.

Set in 16 pt. Plantin by Minnie B. Raven.

Printed in the United States on permanent paper.

Library of Congress Cataloging in Publication Data

Shelton, Gene.
    Texas Horsetrading Co. / Gene Shelton.
      p. cm.
    ISBN 0-7838-8304-8 (lg. print : hc : alk. paper)
    1. Large type books. I. Title.
  [PS3569.H39364T4   1998]
   813′.54—dc21   98-5397

TEXAS
HORSETRADING CO.

ONE

The last thing Brubs McCallan remembered was a beer bottle headed straight for the bridge of his nose.

Now he came awake in a near panic, a cold, numbing fear that he had gone blind. Beyond the stabbing pain in his head he could make out only jerky, hazy shapes.

Brubs sighed with relief as he realized he was only in jail.

The shapes were hazy and indistinct partly because only a thin, weak light filtered into the cell from the low flame of a guttering oil lamp on a shelf outside the bars. And the shapes were fuzzy partly because his left eye was swollen almost shut.

Brubs leaned back against the thin blankets on the hard wooden cot and groaned. The movement sent the sledgehammer in his head to pounding a fresh set of spikes through his temples.

"Good morning."

Brubs started at the sound of the voice. He tried to focus his good eye on the dim form on the cot across the room. He could tell that the man was tall. His boots stuck out past the end of the cot. He had an arm hooked behind his head for a pillow, his hat pulled down over his eyes. "Mornin' yourself," Brubs mumbled over a swollen lower lip. "Question is, which mornin' is it, anyway?"

"Sunday, I believe. How do you feel?"

"Like I had a boot hung up in the stirrup and got drug over half of Texas." Brubs lifted a hand to his puffy face and heard the scratch of his palm against stubble. "And like somebody swabbed the outhouse with my tongue. Other than that, passin' fair."

"Glad to hear that. I was afraid that beer bottle might have caused some permanent damage."

Brubs swung his feet over the edge of the cot, sat up, and immediately regretted it. The hammer slammed harder against the spikes in his brain. He squinted at the tall man on the bunk across the way. "I remember you," he said after a moment. "How come you whopped me with that beer bottle?"

"I couldn't find an ax handle and you were getting the upper hand on me at the time," the man said.

Brubs wiggled his nose between a thumb and forefinger. "At least you didn't bust my beak again," he said. "That would have plumb made me mad. I done broke it twice the last year and a half. What was we fightin' about?"

The tall man swung his feet over the side of the cot and sat, rubbing a hand across the back of his neck. "You don't remember? After all, you started it."

"Oh. Yeah, I reckon it's comin' back now. But that cowboy was cheatin'. Seen him palm a card on his deal." Brubs snorted in disgust. "Wasn't even good at cheatin'."

"How do you know that?"

"If he'd been any good I wouldn't of caught him. I can't play poker worth a flip. Who pulled him off me?"

"I did."

"What'd you do that for? I had him right where I wanted him. I was hittin' him square in the fist with my face ever' time he swung. Another minute or two, I'd of had him wore plumb down."

"I didn't want to interfere, but I saw him reach for a knife. That didn't seem fair in a fist-fight."

Brubs sighed. "You're dead right about that. That when I belted you?"

"The first time."

Brubs heaved himself unsteadily to his feet. It wasn't easy. Brubs packed a hundred and sixty pounds of mostly muscle on a stubby five-foot-seven frame, and it seemed to him that every one of those muscles was bruised, stretched, or sore. Standing up didn't help his head much, either.

The man on the other bunk raised a hand. "If you don't mind, I'd just as soon not start it again. I don't have a beer bottle with me at the moment."

"Aw, hell," Brubs said, "I wasn't gonna start

nothin'. Just wanted to say I'm obliged you didn't let that cowboy stick a knife in my gizzard." He strode stiffly to the side of the bunk and offered a hand. "Brubs McCallan."

The man on the cot stood. He was a head taller than Brubs, lean and wiry, built along the lines of a mountain cat where Brubs tended toward the badger clan. The lanky man took Brubs's hand. His grip was firm and dry. "Dave Willoughby. Nice to make your acquaintance under more civilized conditions."

"Wouldn't call the San Antonio jail civilized," Brubs said with a grin. The smile started his split lower lip to leaking blood again. He released Willoughby's hand. "We tear the place up pretty good?"

"My last recollection is that we had made an impressive start to that end," Willoughby said. "Shortly thereafter, somebody blew the lantern out on me, too."

Both men turned as a door creaked open and bootsteps sounded. The oil lamp outside the cell flared higher as a stocky man twisted the brass key of the wick feeder with a thick hand. The light spilled over a weathered face crowned by an unruly thatch of gray hair. "What's all the yammering about? Gettin' so a man can't sleep around here anymore."

The stocky man stood with the lamp held at shoulder height. A ring of keys clinked as he hobbled to the cell. His left knee was stiff. He had to swing the leg in a half circle when he walked. The lamplight glittered from a badge on his vest and the brass back strap of a big revolver holstered high on his right hip.

"You the sheriff?" Brubs asked.

"Night deputy. Sheriff don't come on duty for another couple hours. Name's Charlie Purvis. If you boys are gonna be the guests of Bexar County for a while, you better learn to keep it quiet when I'm on duty."

"We will certainly keep that in mind, Deputy Purvis," Dave Willoughby said. "We apologize for having disturbed you. We will be more reserved in the future."

Brubs glared through his one open eye at the deputy. "What do you mean, guests of the county?"

"In case you boys ain't heard," the deputy said, "that brawl you started over at the Longhorn just about wrecked the place. I don't figure you two've got enough to pay the fines and damages."

Dave sighed audibly. "How much might that be, Deputy?"

"Twenty-dollar fine apiece for startin' the fight and disturbin' the peace. Thirty-one dollars each for damages. Plus a dime for the beer bottle you busted over your friend's head."

"What?" Brubs's voice was a startled croak. "You gonna charge this man a dime for whoppin' me with a beer bottle?"

The deputy shrugged. "Good glass bottles are hard to find out here. Owner of the Longhorn says they're worth a dime apiece."

Brubs snorted in disgust. "Damnedest thing I ever heard." He glanced up at Willoughby. "Good thing you didn't hit me with the back bar mirror. God knows what that would of cost. You got any money, Dave?"

Willoughby rummaged in a pocket and poked a finger among a handful of coins. "Thirty-one cents."

Brubs sighed in relief. "Good. There for a minute I was afraid we was plumb broke." He fumbled in his own pocket. "I got seventeen cents. Had four dollars when I set in on that poker game."

"Looks like you boys got troubles," Purvis said, shaking his shaggy head. "Can't let you out till the fines and damages are paid."

"How we gonna pay if we're in jail?"

Purvis shrugged. "Should have thought about that before you decided to wreck the Longhorn. Guess you'll just have to work it out on the county farm."

"Farm!" Brubs sniffed in wounded indignation and held out his hands. "These look like farmer's hands?"

The deputy squinted. "Nope. Don't show no sign of work if you don't count the skinned knuckles." Purvis grinned. "They'll toughen up quick on a hoe handle. We got forty acres in corn and cotton, and ten weeds for every crop plant. Pay's four bits a day." He scratched his jaw with a thick finger. "Let's see, now — fifty cents a day, you owe fifty-one dollars. . . . Works out to a hundred and two days. Each."

Dave Willoughby sighed. "Looks like it's going to be a long summer."

Purvis plucked a watch from his vest pocket, flipped the case open, and grunted. "Near onto sunup. You boys wrecked my nap. Might as well put some coffee on." He snapped the watch shut. "I reckon the county can spare a couple cups if you two rowdies want some."

Brubs scrubbed a hand over the back of his neck. "I'll shoot anybody you want for a cup of coffee. Got anything for hangovers? I got a size twelve headache in a size seven head."

The deputy chuckled. "Sympathy's all I got to offer. Know how you feel. I been there, back in my younger days. Busted up a saloon or two myself. You boys sit tight. I'll be back in a few minutes with the coffee."

Brubs trudged back to the cot and sat, elbows propped against his knees. He became aware of a gray light spreading through the cell and glanced at the wall above Dave's bunk. A small, barred rectangle high above the floor brightened with the approaching dawn. "Well, Dave," Brubs said after a moment, "you sure got us in a mess this time."

Willoughby turned to face Brubs, a quizzical expression on his face. "*I* got us in a mess? I was under the impression that you started the fight and I was the innocent bystander."

Brubs shrugged as best he could without moving his throbbing head. "Don't matter. Question now is, how do we break out of here?"

Willoughby raised a hand, palm out. "Wait a minute — you can't be serious! Breaking out of jail is a felony offense. We would be wanted criminals, possibly with a price on our heads. If you're thinking of escape, even if it was possible, count me out."

Brubs prodded his puffy eyebrow with a finger. The swelling seemed to be going down some. "I ain't working for the county, Dave. 'Specially not on some damn farm." He squinted at his free hand. "These hands don't fit no hoe handle. That's how come I left home in the first place."

Willoughby strode to his own bunk and stretched out on his back. "Where's home?"

"Nacogdoches, I reckon. Never had a real home to call it such." He raised his undamaged eyebrow at Willoughby. "You sure talk funny. Since we're tradin' life stories here, where you from?"

"Cincinnati."

"That on the Sabine or the Red River?"

"Neither. It's on the Ohio."

Brubs moaned. "Oh, Christ. I'm sittin' here tryin' my best to die from day-old whiskey, I got my butt whopped in a saloon fight, I owe money I ain't got, I been threatened with choppin' cotton, and now it turns out I'm sharin' a cell with a Yankee. If I hadn't had such a damn good time last night, I'd be plumb disgusted."

14

A faint smile flitted over Willoughby's face. "I suppose it was a rather interesting diversion, at that." He winced and probed the inside of his cheek with his tongue. "I think you chipped one of my teeth. For a little man, you swing a mean punch."

The creak of the door between cell block and outer office brought both men to their feet. Brubs could smell the coffee before the deputy came into view, carrying two tin cups on a flat wooden slab. Purvis crouched stiffly and slid the cups through the grub slot of the cell.

Brubs grabbed a cup, scorched his fingers on the hot tin, sipped at the scalding liquid, and sighed, contented. "Mother's milk for a child with a hangover," he said. "If I was a preacher I'd bless your soul, Charlie Purvis."

Purvis straightened slowly, the creak of his joints clearly audible. "You boys'll get some half-raw bacon and burnt biscuits when the sheriff gets here. Need anything else meantime?"

"I don't reckon you could see your way clear to leave the key in the lock?" Brubs asked hopefully.

Purvis shook his head. "Couldn't do that." He pointed toward a dark smear on the adobe wall near the door of the office. "Just in case you boys got some ideas perkin' along with the headaches, study on that spot over there. That's what's left of the last man tried to bust out of my jail." He clucked his tongue. "Sure did hate to cut down on him with that smoothbore. Double load of buckshot splattered guts all over the place. Made a downright awful mess. Why, pieces of that fellow were —"

"I think we understand your message, Deputy," Willoughby interrupted with a wince. "If you don't mind, spare us the gory details."

The deputy shrugged. "Well, I'll leave you boys to your chicken pluckin'. Sure don't envy you none. It gets hotter than the devil's kitchen out in those fields in summer."

Brubs moaned aloud at the comment.

"Is there somebody who could help us?" Willoughby asked. "A bondsman, perhaps, or someone who would loan us the money to get out of here?"

Charlie Purvis frowned. "Might be one man. I'm not sure you'd like the deal, though."

"Charlie," Brubs said, pleading, "I'd make a deal with Old Scratch himself to keep my hands off a damn hoe handle."

The deputy shrugged. "Same difference, maybe. But I'll talk to him." Purvis turned and limped away. The door creaked shut behind him.

Brubs stopped pacing the narrow cell and glanced at the small, high window overhead, then at the lean man reclining on the bunk. "How long we been in this place, Dave?"

Willoughby shoved the hat back from over his eyes. "I'd guess a little over half a day."

"Seems a passel longer than that."

"Patience, I gather, is not your strong suit."

16

Brubs snorted. "Buzzards got patience. All it gets 'em is rotten meat and a yard and a half of ugly apiece." He started pacing again.

"Relax, Brubs," Willoughby said, "you're wasting energy and tiring me out, tromping back and forth like that." He pulled the hat back over his eyes. "Better save your strength for that cotton patch."

Brubs paused to glare at the man on the cot. "You are truly a comfort to a dyin' man, Dave Willoughby. Truly a comfort."

The clomp of boots and the squeak of the door brought Brubs's pacing to a halt. Sheriff Milt Garrison strode to the cell, a big, burly man at his side. The big man seemed to wear more hair than a grizzly, Brubs thought. Gray fur covered most of his face, bristled his forearms, sprouted from heavy knuckles, and even stuck out through the buttonholes on his shirt. For a moment Brubs thought the man didn't have any eyes. Then he realized they were the same color as the hair and were tucked back under brows as thick and wiry as badger bristles.

"These the two Charlie told me about?" The hairy man's voice grated like a shovel blade against gravel.

"That's them." Milt Garrison leaned against the bars of the cell. "Told you they didn't look like much."

"Well, hell," the hairy one said, "if they're tough enough to wreck the Longhorn, maybe they'll do."

17

"Boys, meet Lawrence T. Pettibone, owner of Bexar and Rio Grande Freight Lines. He's got a deal to offer you." Garrison waved a hand toward the prisoners. "The short one's Brubs McCallan. Other one's Dave Willoughby."

Lawrence T. Pettibone nodded a greeting. "I hear you boys run up a pretty big bill last night. How bad you want to get shut of this place?"

"Mighty bad, Mr. Pettibone," Brubs said.

"All right, here's the deal. I won't say it but once, so you listen careful." Pettibone's smoky eyes seemed to turn harder, like a prize agate marble Brubs remembered from his childhood. "I need two men. You boys got horses and saddles?"

Brubs nodded. "Yes, sir, Mr. Pettibone, we sure do. Over at the livery."

Pettibone snorted. "Probably owe money on them, too."

"Yes, sir. I reckon we owe a dollar apiece board on the mounts."

"You savvy guns?"

Brubs nodded again. "Sure do. I'm a better'n fair hand with a long gun, and I can hit an outhouse with a pistol if it ain't too far off."

"How about you, Willoughby?"

Willoughby's brow wrinkled. "Yes, sir, I can use weapons. If the need arises." His tone sounded cautious.

Pettibone grunted. Brubs couldn't tell if it was a good grunt or a bad grunt. "All right, I guess you two'll do. I was hopin' for better, but a man can't be too picky these days." He pulled a twist of tobacco from a shirt pocket, gnawed off a chew, and settled it in his cheek. "I need two outriders. Guards for a shipment goin' to El Paso day after tomorrow. I'll pay your fines and damages. You ride shotgun for the Bexar and Rio line until you work it off. At a dollar a day."

Brubs sighed in relief. "Dave, that's twice the pay the county offered. And no hoe handles."

"Mr. Pettibone," Willoughby said, "may I inquire as to why you are short of manpower?"

Pettibone twisted his head and spat a wad of tobacco juice. It spanged neatly into a brass cuspidor below the lamp shelf. "Bandits killed 'em last run. Blew more holes in 'em than we could count. Stole my whole damn load."

"Bandits? You mean outlaws?"

Pettibone sighed in disgust. "Now just who the hell else would hold up a freight wagon? A gang of Methodist preachers?"

Willoughby shook his head warily. "I'm not sure about this, Mr. Pettibone. It's one thing to work for a man. It's another matter to possibly have to kill or be killed in the line of work."

Pettibone's gray eyes narrowed. "Suit yourself, son. It don't matter to me. But I need *two* men. Charlie said he figured you two come as a package. Guess I'll have to find me a couple other saddle tramps." He turned and started to walk away.

"Mr. Pettibone, wait a minute," Brubs called. He turned to Dave. "You leave the talkin' to

19

me, Dave," he whispered. "I'm gettin' out of here, and you're goin' with me."

The big man turned back.

"My partner here ain't no lace-drawers type violet, Mr. Pettibone," Brubs said earnestly. "He's a top hand with a gun and got more guts than a bull buffalo. He just went through some stuff in the war that bothers him time to time. Don't you fret about old Dave." He clapped his cell mate on the shoulder. "You just get us out of here, and we'll make sure your wagon gets through."

Pettibone glared at the two prisoners for several heartbeats, then shrugged. "All right. You're hired." He jabbed a heavy finger at Brubs. "I want you boys to know one thing. I ain't in the charity business. You duck out or turn yellow on me and you'll wish to high hell you were back in this lockup, 'cause I'll skin you out and tan your hides for a pillow to ease my piles, and every time I go to the outhouse I'll take it along to remember you by. Savvy?"

"Yes, sir," Brubs said eagerly, "we savvy. You're the boss."

"Good. Keep that in mind. I'll pick you boys up tomorrow afternoon." He turned to walk away.

"Mr. Pettibone?"

"Now what, McCallan?"

Brubs swallowed. "Reckon you could get us out today? No disrespect to Bexar County or this fine sheriff here, but this ain't the most com-

20

fortable jail I ever been in. I sure would like to get my stuff in shape and take the kinks out of my sorrel before we move out."

Pettibone glowered at Brubs for a moment. "Damned if you boys don't try a man's patience something fierce. All right, I'll get you out now. You got any place to stay?"

"No, sir, Mr. Pettibone."

Pettibone's massive chest rose and fell. Brubs thought he saw the hair in the big man's ears bristle. "You can bunk in at my place. Cost you a dollar a day apiece. I'll add it onto what it's going to cost me to spring the pair of you. Damn, but the cost of help's gettin' high these days." Pettibone turned to the sheriff. "Cut 'em loose, Milt."

Brubs heaved a deep sigh of relief as the key turned in the cell lock and the barred door swung open. He knew it was the same air outside the cell as in, but it still smelled better. He and Willoughby fell into step behind the sheriff and Pettibone.

Brubs and Willoughby waited patiently as Lawrence T. Pettibone frowned at the column of figures on Sheriff Milt Garrison's ledger. "What the hell's this ten cents for a beer bottle?"

"Dave busted one over my head, Mr. Pettibone," Brubs said.

Pettibone snorted in disgust. "Damnedest thing I ever heard," he growled. "Chargin' a man for bustin' a beer bottle in a saloon brawl."

"Sort of the way I figured it, Mr. Pettibone,"

Brubs said earnestly. "Pricin' a man's fun plumb out of sight these days."

"I ain't payin' for no damn bottle," Pettibone said. "No way I can figure how to get ten cents worth of work out of two guys on a dollar a day."

Brubs dug in a pocket and produced a coin. "Give me a nickel, Dave. We'll split the cost of the bottle."

Pettibone finally grunted and pulled a wad of bills from his pocket. Brubs's eyes went wide at the sight of the roll. It was more money than he'd seen in one place since the big horse race up in Denton. Pettibone licked a thumb and counted out the bills, sighing as he caressed each one. Pettibone acted like he was burying a sainted mother every time he put a dollar on the desk, Brubs thought.

Garrison gathered up the bills, dropped the money in a tin box, and scribbled a receipt. He handed the paper to Pettibone, then retrieved the prisoners' weapons from a locked closet. "Guess you bought yourself some shotgun riders, Lawrence," he said.

Pettibone cast a cold glance at Brubs and Willoughby. "Don't know if I bought a good horse or a wind-broke plug," he groused. "I sure as hell hope they ride and shoot better than they smell. You boys are a touch ripe. There's a big water tank out by my wagon barn. Wouldn't hurt either of you to nuzzle up to some soap. Now, strap them gun belts on and let's go bail your horses out of the lockup."

Willoughby paused for a moment, rotated the cylinder of his Colt, and raised an eyebrow. "Should we go ahead and load the chambers now, Mr. Pettibone?" he asked.

Pettibone groaned aloud. "Fools. I just bought two idiots with my hard-earned money. Dammit, son, what good's an unloaded pistol?" He watched in disgust as Willoughby thumbed cartridges into the Colt and reached for his Winchester rifle. "I guess you boys got plenty of ammunition?"

"I got ten rifle cartridges," Brubs said, shoving loads into his scarred Henry .44 rimfire long gun. "Maybe a dozen for the pistol."

"I have half a box of .44-40's," Willoughby said. "Same caliber fits both my handgun and rifle."

Pettibone snorted in disgust. "Damn. Now I've got to lay out some more hard cash on you two. My men don't ride with less than a hundred rounds each. Come on — we'll stop off at the general store down the street."

The two men fell into step behind Pettibone. A few minutes later the hairy one emerged from the store, four boxes of ammunition in a big hand. "I'll add the cost of the shells to your bill, boys. Fifty cents a box."

"Fifty cents? Mr. Pettibone, that's a dime more than I paid anywhere," Brubs said, incredulous.

"Call it a nuisance fee," Pettibone growled,

"because you boys are nuisances if I ever seen 'em. Course, if you'd rather work it out with the county —"

"No, sir," Brubs said quickly. "I reckon that's fair enough. We won't nuisance you no more."

"I doubt that." Pettibone spat a wad of used-up tobacco into the street. "Let's get home before you two drifters cost me my last dollar."

"Mr. Pettibone?"

"What now, McCallan?"

"Any chance we could get a bottle of whiskey added to our bill?"

"No, by God!" Pettibone bellowed. "Don't push your luck, boy, or you'll be behind a hoe handle all summer!"

"Yes, sir," Brubs said. "But it was worth a try."

A half hour later, Brubs and Willoughby rode side by side behind Lawrence T. Pettibone's buggy. Brubs forked a big, rangy sorrel, and Dave rode a leggy black that looked to have some Tennessee racing stock in his bloodline.

"Brubs," Willoughby said quietly, "I have the distinct impression that our new employer is somewhat thrifty with his funds."

Brubs flashed a quick grin. "I reckon he can squeeze a peso until the Mexican eagle looks like a plucked crow."

Lawrence T. Pettibone's combination home and wagon yard and adjoining stock pastures spread over most of a section on the northern outskirts of San Antonio.

Brubs had to admit he was impressed. The corrals were sturdy, fenced by peeled logs the size of a man's thigh, and watered by a big windmill that creaked as it whirred in the southwest breeze. The barn was as solidly built as the corrals, expansive and well-ventilated. The main house was big, and built of real cut lumber, not adobe or split logs.

Brubs was even more impressed with what came from inside the big house.

Pettibone pushed the door open, growled at Brubs and Willoughby to wait on the porch, and went inside. He was back a minute later with a stiff-bristled brush and a bar of lye soap in hand, and one of the prettiest girls Brubs had seen west of Savannah trailing behind.

The girl was blonde. Palomino hair tumbled past her shoulders, dancing gold in the warm afternoon sunshine. The pale rose housedress she wore wrapped itself around a figure that made Brubs want to paw the ground and snort. Her eyes were big, blue, and had a smoldering look about them above a perky, upturned nose. She looked to be about twenty. This, Brubs knew instinctively, was one hot-blooded woman. He swept the battered and stained hat from his head.

"Boys, this here is Callie, my daughter," Pettibone said. "Callie, these two bums'll be riding shotgun for us a spell. Don't shoot 'em for

25

prowlers until I get my money back out of 'em. The little feller's name is Brubs McCallan. The tall one's Dave Willoughby."

Brubs bowed deep at the waist, then grinned at the blonde. He wished for a moment he had just had a bath and shave; some women were mighty picky about that, as if it made some sort of difference. "Mighty pleased to make your acquaintance, Miss Pettibone," Brubs said. "A pretty girl does brighten a poor saddle tramp's day."

"Lay a hand on Callie and I'll kill you," Pettibone said. It wasn't exactly a threat, Brubs noted. More like a statement of fact.

Brubs tore his gaze from the girl and glanced at his cell mate. Willoughby had removed his hat, but merely nodded a greeting. He did not speak.

A second woman, a Mexican somewhere in her late twenties, appeared at the door. She was a bit thick of hip and waist, her upper lip dusted by scattered but distinct black hairs. Overall though, not bad looking, Brubs decided. Away from the blonde she might even be pretty.

"That's Juanita. She's the cook and maid." Pettibone held out the brush and lye soap. "Long as I'm makin' introductions, this is stuff to clean up with. Put your horses in the barn and yourselves in that water tank out back, or don't come in for supper."

Brubs hesitated, reluctant to leave the warm glow that seemed to spread in all directions from

26

Callie, until he realized that Lawrence T. Pettibone was glaring a hole through him. Brubs
quickly replaced his hat, turned away, and
mounted with a flourish, swinging into the saddle without touching a stirrup. He wasn't above
showing off a bit when a pretty girl was watching. He kneed his sorrel gelding around and set
off after Willoughby, who was already leading
his leggy black toward the barn thirty yards
away.

"Man, ain't she something?" Brubs said as he
reined in alongside Willoughby. "I ain't seen a
filly like that my whole life through. Prime stuff,
that Callie."

Willoughby cast a worried glance at Brubs.
"You heard what Pettibone said, Brubs. You'd
better leave the girl alone."

Brubs chuckled aloud. "Just adds a little spice
to the puddin', my Yankee friend. You see the
way Callie was lookin' at me? Her eyes got all
smoky-like."

"I saw the way Pettibone was looking at you."
Willoughby swung the corral gate open.

"Ah, that inflated tadpole ain't much to worry
about," Brubs said.

"I worry about a lot of things, Brubs. One of
which is that if you try messing around with that
girl, somebody is likely to get hurt. Like you and
me."

Brubs reached down and cuffed Dave on the
shoulder. "Don't you fret, Dave. You just watch
ol' Brubs work that herd, you'll learn somethin'

about handlin' women."

"And that," Willoughby said solemnly, "is exactly what's bothering me. I'm beginning to wonder if perhaps Brubs McCallan wasn't put on this earth just to get one Dave Willoughby killed."

TWO

Brubs McCallan leaned against the corral fence and worried a frayed toothpick with his tongue as he stared toward the Pettibone house. He sighed wistfully.

"That's her room, Dave," he said, as the soft breeze fluttered the window curtains in a lower floor corner room.

Dave Willoughby squatted beside a fence post, watching a dung beetle try to roll a ball of horse manure up the steep, sandy incline of a drainage ditch. Dave glanced up at Brubs. "Maybe I did hit you too hard with that beer bottle," he said. "Or maybe you just didn't have too many brains before. Forget the girl, Brubs. She's trouble."

Brubs rolled the toothpick from one corner of his mouth to the other and grinned at Willoughby. "Partner, you got to learn how to read sign on women. I can tell by the way Callie watched me all through supper she's loco for Brubs McCallan. And that Juanita's got an itch for you, Dave. Seen it in her eyes, too, but you just set there like a fly on a horse apple. How come you don't talk much around females?"

Willoughby removed his hat and ran his fingers through his thick brown hair. "I've always been a little reserved around women," he said.

"Never can seem to think of the right words." He canted an eyebrow at Brubs. "Do me a favor. Leave me completely out of your plans for any amorous adventures involving Lawrence T. Pettibone's daughter. That old man would kill you for sure. And since he considers us a pair, he might decide to shoot me, too, on general principle."

"Dave Willoughby," Brubs said with a solemn shake of the head, "you are the most down-in-the-mouth, pessimistic Yankee I done ever met. Man listened to you, he never would get no spice in his life."

"Some spice can tear up a man's stomach." Willoughby fell silent for a moment, staring at the bug. "I've been watching this insect. I think there's a message here for us, Brubs. The beetle has been trying to roll that ball of manure up the incline for fifteen minutes, pushing with his back legs and with his head downslope, and he hasn't gained more than three inches."

Brubs chuckled. "Like a pair of saddle tramps. The bug starts out ankle deep in corral droppin's, works hisself to a frazzle, goes at everything backasswards, and when he gets to where he's goin' he's got nothin' but a turd for his troubles. Cowboy's life in a nutshell, right there. And we ain't a damn bit smarter than that tumblebug."

Willoughby cast a quick glance at Brubs. "An astute bit of philosophy, my friend. *Dictum sapienti sat est.*"

"What kind of lingo is that?"

"Latin. It translates as, 'What's been said is enough for anyone with sense.' Roman dramatist named Plautus wrote it."

Brubs frowned. "Didn't know they had cowboys in Rome. Damned if you don't talk funnier all the time, Dave. I got to work on that one awhile." He plucked the toothpick from his mouth and tossed it aside. "I knew some Latins once. Mexicans, really. I speak a little Mex, but it don't sound a whole lot like that there Latin." Brubs abruptly pushed himself away from the fence. "Now what the blue-eyed thunder is this?"

A lean young man clad entirely in black strode toward the corral. Silver conchas flashed sunlight from his hatband and the gun belt around his hips. He carried a Colt Peacemaker strapped low on his right thigh. He stopped a few feet from Brubs.

"You two the new outriders?" It was as much a challenge as a question.

"Reckon so," Brubs said casually.

"My name's Brazos," the young man said. "I expect you recognize the name."

Brubs's brow furrowed. "Can't say as I do. Well, I did know a wolfer once up on the Red went by that name, but he was older'n the river when I met him. Married to the ugliest Papago squaw the Great Spirit ever put on earth. Reckon you're not him. I'm Brubs McCallan. This here's Dave Willoughby."

31

"I've killed four men."

"That a fact?"

"Fair, stand-up fights. Some say I'm the fastest gun in Texas." The dark eyes in the thin face narrowed. "You boys gunmen? I don't ride with anybody who can't use a Colt."

Brubs leaned back against the fence, folded his arms across his chest, and grinned. "Me, I'm a rifle shooter myself. Dave here's the *pistolero*. Pure poison with a handgun —"

"Brubs —"

"Quickest hand and sharpest eye I ever seen," Brubs continued, shaking his head in awe. "Like a rattler and an eagle. Lost track of the fast guns old Dave's put down."

"Brubs —"

Brazos shifted his weight and stared through narrowed eyelids at Dave. "Never heard of a gunfighter by that name. How fast are you, Willoughby?"

"Now, wait a minute! Brubs —"

Brubs waved a hand. "Easy, partner. Don't go gettin' yourself all lathered up. I know how easy you get plumb killin' mad all over sometimes."

"Brubs, for Christ's sake —"

"Now, listen to me, Dave. There ain't no need to shoot Brazos. We just might could use that gun of his before we get to El Paso. Besides, gun shootin' might spook Mr. Pettibone's mules. We sure don't want to rile that old grizzly bear."

Brazos settled back on his heels and stared at Willoughby, indecision in his black eyes. Then

32

he shrugged. "I suppose McCallan's right. We'll find out how good you are if we run across that bunch of bandits out there." The young man turned and strode away. It seemed to Brubs that Brazos walked away a lot faster than he walked up.

"Brubs McCallan," Willoughby said, his tone tight and angry, "when are you going to start keeping your mouth shut? That man could have killed me!"

Brubs shrugged. "All spit and no tobacco to that one. Didn't have them cold killer's eyes. Besides, you could of took him."

"Took him?" Willoughby's tone was a mixture of bewilderment and outrage. "In a gunfight? Me, a man whose fastest draw takes most of February? You are totally out of your mind. How did you know he wouldn't pull on me?"

"Didn't. But if he had, I'd of shot him."

Willoughby moaned aloud. "To borrow one of your own phrases, that knowledge is truly a comfort to me, Brubs."

Brubs clapped his friend on the shoulder. "Why, amigo, I expect you'd do the same for me. Nothin' hurt. Sun's goin' down. Let's turn in."

Lawrence T. Pettibone stood with his hands on his hips, a scowl on his hairy face, and let his heavy gaze linger for a moment on the face of each man in the wagon yard.

A draft horse snorted dust from its nostrils

and shook its head, rattling the harness. Two Studebaker freight wagons each with a six-horse hitch, sat heavy on their running gear. The sun was barely above the eastern horizon.

"All right, you honyocks," Pettibone finally said, "this shipment's ready to move. I ain't got to tell you I expect it to get to El Paso in one piece. If it don't, you can give your hearts to the Lord 'cause I'm takin' your butts." He paused for a moment for emphasis. "I'd go myself if I wasn't stove up with rheumatics in this bum hip. I built this damn freight line with my own hands and my own sweat, but now I got to trust somebody else to do the work. And there's six months' worth of my time and my money on those wagons."

Brubs only half listened. He was looking past Pettibone's shoulder toward the ground-floor corner window of the big house. He was sure he saw the curtains flutter. That meant Callie was watching. Brubs squared his shoulders, lifted the fingertips of his free hand to his hat brim, and dipped his head in a quick nod toward the window. He figured it wouldn't hurt a thing to let her know he knew she was watching. The sorrel gelding snorted, spraying snot over Brubs's shirtsleeve.

"Now," Pettibone said, "I hear stories that there's more than just white bandits out there. Word is some bronco Cherry Cows busted off the reservation. Plus our usual gaggle of Mexican thieves. Keep a sharp watch out. You boys

34

got your assignments, so quit wastin' my time and money and earn your keep. I'll see you back here in a few weeks." He paused for a heartbeat, then added, "I damn well *better* see you back here."

The freight line owner turned and stalked back toward the house, big boots puffing dust as he walked.

Two burly drivers climbed into the wagon seats, picked up reins, and started barking curses at the draft horses. The animals leaned into the leather and the wagons jolted into motion. The small caravan lined out as Dave and Brubs mounted.

A crusty old buffalo hunter called John Blue took the left point of the lead wagon, his shoulders hunched over the saddle horn. Brazos had the right point, the sun glittering off even more silver conchas studded to his saddle and bridle headstall. Brazos was already practicing his fast draw, whipping the Colt from its cutaway holster and pointing it first at one object, then another.

Mort Freeman, the driver of the second wagon, stared in disgust at Brazos for a moment, then spat. "Damn fool kid and his silver spots. Might as well send up smoke tellin' everybody where we're at. Be lucky if we make it past the first bend in the road without gettin' jumped."

Willoughby cast a quick glance at the brawny teamster with the tobacco-stained beard. "Is it really that dangerous out there, Mr. Freeman?"

"Like a rattler on a hot stove." He yelled an

oath at the off-wheel horse; the big bay flinched and settled in to haul against the traces.

Willoughby kneed his horse closer to Brubs's sorrel. "What's a Cherry Cow?"

Brubs cocked an eyebrow at Willoughby. "Amigo, you're greener'n May grass after a good rain. Cherry Cows is what us Texans call Chiricahua Apaches. Bad Injuns. Their idea of a good time's to cut a man's eyelids off and stake him out face up in the sun. And *that's* when they're feelin' generous toward their fellow man."

Willoughby winced. "What happens if they jump us?"

Brubs flashed a quick grin. "Don't worry about it, partner. I got a feelin' about this trip. Gonna be just a nice, peaceful ride through the countryside."

The two rode in silence for a few yards, Willoughby's brow creased by a deep frown, concern mirrored in his blue eyes.

"What's gnawin' at your gut, buddy?" Brubs finally asked.

"Just wondering," Willoughby said solemnly, "if it's too late to go back to jail."

Sweat trickled down Brubs McCallan's neck and turned the coat of dust on his cotton shirt into watery smudges of thin mud. The spring sun hammered down with an intensity that promised a scorching summer ahead.

He twisted in the saddle to survey the countryside. Five days and nearly a hundred miles out of San Antonio, the country had changed. The road they followed now twisted through rolling, sandy hills dotted with clumps of chaparral and mesquite. Scattered bunchgrass battled for space and moisture with prickly pear and bush cactus. Sand swirled along the parched ground, stirred by a southwest wind as hot and dry as the Sonoran Desert.

Five days, and so far the most dangerous things they had seen were scorpions and rattlesnakes. Brubs's eyes itched from the steady barrage of sand and wind; his throat was as parched as the countryside. He would have sold at least a share of his soul for a cold beer.

Brubs watched through a break in the mesquite as, two hundred yards ahead, Brazos suddenly wheeled his mount from atop a low ridge and raced back toward the wagons.

Brubs slipped his rifle from the saddle scabbard, cracked the action to make sure a round was chambered, then kneed his horse forward.

"What is it, Brazos?" Brubs heard the wariness in John Blue's words. The old man already had his rifle, a scarred Sharps Fifty, in hand and cocked.

"Big dust cloud just over the rise up ahead," Brazos said. His eyes were wide and his face pale where sweat had washed away the dust. "It looks like an army on the move out there."

Brubs heard the thump of hooves as Willoughby loped his mount up alongside. "What's going on?" Willoughby had his Winchester unsheathed and ready, the stock resting on his right thigh.

"We're fixing to find out," John Blue said. "You boys come with me. Look sharp."

Brubs felt the first worm of worry wriggle in his gut as he kneed the sorrel to keep pace with Blue's wiry little Mexican-type roan.

All four men pulled their mounts to a stop atop the ridge. Hundreds of horses, scattered into numerous groups, moved along at a brisk trot in the near distance. Most of them were small, wiry-muscled animals, with long manes and tails that whipped in the wind. Every horse color imaginable seemed to be there, from blacks to zebra duns to paints to sorrels and browns and even a couple that looked to be pure white. Here and there a taller horse stood out among one of the bands.

"Mustangs," John Blue said. "Headed for water, most likely. Don't seem overly spooked."

Brubs heard Willoughby's low whistle and felt a twinge of excitement himself; he had heard of the big bands of wild horses for years, had even seen a dozen or so mustangs in the distance a couple of times — at least he had seen their rear ends as they topped a distant ridge or rounded a bend in a river.

"Are those all wild horses?" Willoughby's soft question held more than a touch of awe.

"Sure are, son," John Blue said. "I been riding through and around mustangs most of my life, and I don't recollect ever seeing this many on the move at one time." He lowered the hammer of the Sharps Fifty and thrust the weapon back into the saddle boot, but never took his gaze from the horses.

"Who owns them?" Willoughby asked.

"Nobody." The old-timer sighed wistfully. "We may be looking at the last really free critters on this earth. Someday, I guess they'll be gone, too, like the buffalo. I'll miss 'em." His shoulders seemed to slump even more as the mustangs disappeared from view. "Back to work, boys. We've got several miles to cover before we hit water, and I'm tired of dry camps."

Brubs McCallan leaned back against his bedroll and stared toward the stars emerging in the darkening sky above. The wind had dropped at sundown. With the dying breeze, the dust haze began to settle. Soon the sky would be clear, the stars a blanket across the deep blue-black night.

Brubs was content. His belly was full — not the best meal he'd ever had, but old John Blue was about as good a hand with a skillet as he was with horses. Lawrence T. Pettibone might be a skinflint, but he did lay in some good grub for his teamster crews. And tonight, he and Willoughby didn't have to stand watch until a couple hours before sunup. This camp was a good one, the best yet.

At Brubs's side, Willoughby lay on his bedroll, arms folded behind his head, staring at the sky. The western horizon still showed a faint red-gold swatch, the remnants of a particularly spectacular sunset.

"Brubs," Willoughby said softly, "you mentioned back in jail that you'd served in the war. What did you do during the conflict?"

Brubs grinned. "Kept my butt down and my head lower than that, most times. Never did cotton much to gettin' shot at."

"Nor did I. What regiment were you with?"

"Hood's Brigade. Out of Texas."

"Cavalry?"

"Nope," Brubs said. "They found out I could ride, so naturally they put me in the infantry. Walked through the whole damn war. You?"

"First Ohio Volunteers."

"Oh, Christ," Brubs said with a mock grimace of disgust. "I'm stuck with a genuine blue-leg Yankee for a partner. And a *volunteer* at that."

"You didn't volunteer?"

"Nope. I was one of them conscripts shanghaied a bit after the war broke out. Big, mean-lookin' sergeant said I had me three choices. Join a Confederate outfit and fight Yanks, sign up in the Home Guard and fight Comanches, or get the stuffin's stomped outta me personal by that sergeant." Brubs shrugged. "I knowed Comanches some and figured fightin' Yankees'd be a damn sight easier. Wasn't too keen on tacklin' that sergeant, neither, so I joined Hood's outfit." He glanced at Willoughby. "You fork a horse fair enough. You cavalry?"

Willoughby shook his head. "Artillery. Naturally, since I didn't know a thing about cannons, they put me in charge of a battery of six-pounders."

"Figures," Brubs said. "Take a man can do somethin' pretty good and tell him to do somethin' he can't. Damn wonder either side won the war."

Willoughby sighed. "It's been that way since Hannibal's time, I guess."

"Don't remember hearing about this Hannibal. What outfit was he with?"

Willoughby cast a sideways glance at Brubs. "His war was a long time back. I read about him in history books."

"Seems to me like you read a lot of stuff."

"I've spent most of my life with a book in my hand," Willoughby said. "I was in college, at William and Mary, when the war broke out. Studied history and philosophy."

Brubs shook his head in mock dismay. "Damn me if it don't get worse. Now I got me a college boy *and* a blue-leg Yankee for a saddle partner. Reckon that's why you talk funny. How'd you wind up in Texas?"

Willoughby paused for a moment, then sighed. "It's a long story. Mostly, it was because I got tired of fighting with my folks. I drifted about some up north after the war but didn't find anything that interested me. Then I decided that since I hadn't seen Texas, I might as well take a look."

"Like what you see?"

Willoughby flashed a wry grin. "Except for the fact that everything out here either sticks, stings, or stinks, that I've been in jail for the first time in my life, that I'm flat broke and riding with an ex-Rebel who's trying his best to get me killed, I guess I like it fine."

Brubs laughed aloud. "Aw, hell, Dave. I don't know where you got this crazy idea I'm tryin' to get you killed."

"Are you jackasses going to bed," Mort Freeman yelled from his bedroll beneath the wagon, "or you going to stay awake and bray all night?"

"Just tryin' to convince my amigo here there ain't nothin' gonna happen on this trip, Mort," Brubs replied.

"Well, save your wind." Freeman's canvas groundsheet crackled as he shifted his weight. "If he's spooked, he's smarter than you are. We've got Sour Water Crossing coming up tomorrow. Was I going to hit a couple wagons, that's where I'd do it."

Brubs McCallan could see where the place called Sour Water Crossing might set Mort Freeman's back teeth to itching.

He eased his big sorrel onto the rise overlooking the streambed. Sour Water Creek was a deep gash in the otherwise gently rugged land, and the crossing was the only spot for miles around where heavy wagons could ford the gouge in the earth, Mort had said. Brubs knew at a glance the big teamster was right.

42

The trail ahead twisted through a stand of scraggly cottonwoods, snaked a narrow path through a jumble of fallen trees and small sandstone boulders, then angled up the steep bank on the west side of the dry creek bed. Two dead cottonwoods lay in the creek, the heavy trunk of one blocking the wagon road. Brubs figured it must have been carried there in a recent flash flood. Bits and pieces of drift trash hung in the lower limbs of the standing trees and traced a ragged line along the walls of the creek. The drift line told Brubs that Sour Water Creek wasn't always a dry wash; in a flash flood that could follow one of West Texas' boomer storms, water could be twenty feet deep in the middle of the channel.

He scanned the rugged, rocky hills around the crossing, saw nothing, and watched as Brazos and John Blue kneed their horses toward a deadfall in the trail on the far bank. The two sat in their saddles for a moment, talking, their heads twisting one way and then the other. Finally, John Blue dismounted and crouched to slip the loop of his braided rawhide riata around the trunk of the tree obstructing the road. Brazos remained in the saddle, his hand near the grips of the Colt on his hip.

Brubs glanced around at the sound of hooves approaching at a trot. Dave Willoughby's brow furrowed as his gaze flitted first one way and then the other along the dry wash.

"I don't like the looks of this," Willoughby

said quietly. He slipped his Winchester from the scabbard and racked a round into the chamber.

"Aw, Dave, you're just like an old mama hen in chicken hawk country," Brubs said with a quick grin. "Seein' boogers in ever' shadow. Gonna make me nervous, you don't quit mouthin' the bit like a green-broke bronc. What's got your flanks all a-quiver this time?"

Willoughby nodded toward the tree in the wagon road, his eyes narrowed. "I don't know how Texas trees fall, but back East they don't drop the way that one's lying."

Brubs started to josh the Yankee a bit, but changed his mind in a hurry. Now that Willoughby mentioned it, something didn't feel right about this. Brubs slid his rifle from the scabbard and eared back the hammer. At the corner of his vision he saw the glint of sunlight on steel.

"Watch it!" Brubs yelled.

A split second later he heard the sickening whop of lead against flesh, then the ear-rattling blast of big-bore rifles. One of the wheel horses in the lead wagon screamed and went down, thrashing in the traces; John Blue flopped faceup in the creek bed, half his head gone. The teamster in the lead wagon started to jump free and was cut down under the thunder of a half dozen rifles. The sorrel spooked and danced sideways as Brubs slapped the Henry to his shoulder and fired at a billow of gray-white powder smoke on the far ridge. The shot went wild. At the edge of his vision Brubs saw Mort Freeman's body jerk. The big man tumbled over the wagon seat out of sight. At Brubs's side, Willoughby's Winchester cracked.

A slug buzzed past Brubs's ear and whopped into a cottonwood. Another kicked sand and gravel beside the spooked sorrel's front feet. Brubs caught a glimpse of Willoughby, dismounted now, aiming and firing calmly at the far wall of the ridge. Brubs swung from the saddle, snubbed the reins tight around his wrist, jacked a fresh round into the rifle — and snapped a curse as a horseman came tearing toward them, his mount at a dead run. Brazos's rifle was still in its scabbard, the Colt in its holster, his body hunched over the saddle horn. The kid's eyes looked as big as horse's hooves as he charged past, almost running Dave down.

Brubs caught a glimpse of movement in the rocks downstream and slapped a quick shot, then levered three more blindly toward the thickest haze of powder smoke. The hammer of Willoughby's Winchester clicked on an empty chamber. Brubs reached out and grabbed Willoughby by the shirtsleeve. "Mount up!" he yelled. "We got to get out of here!"

"Those men down there —"

A slug cracked past Brubs's neck. "Dammit, Dave, they're dead! We can't help 'em none. Mount up before they shoot our horses!"

Willoughby swung into the saddle. Brubs's

sorrel spun under him and was in a dead run away from the gunfire before Brubs settled into the saddle. Slugs whipped between the two riders, one humming so close that Brubs winced and ducked. It seemed to Brubs that the rain of lead was like a hailstorm before the two riders topped the ridge and raced out of rifle range. They rode for a mile, spurring hard, before Brubs turned to Willoughby. "You hit?" Brubs yelled.

"Don't think so! You?"

"Not so's I can tell it! Rein in a bit! We got to ease up on these horses or we'll be afoot."

It took another thirty yards to ease the heaving and lathered mounts to a stop. Willoughby's horse had a shallow bullet crease across one hip. A chunk of leather and hardwood as big as a man's thumb was gouged from the swell of Brubs's saddle. He stared at the damage for a couple of heartbeats, his blood chilled. A couple of inches to the right and the women would have been safe from Brubs McCallan forever. It was the only time Brubs could ever remember being happy with a near miss.

Brubs fumbled in a saddlebag, found a box of .44 rimfire ammunition, and started thumbing the stubby cartridges into the loading port of the rifle. His fingers trembled a bit. "You sure you're all right, Dave?"

"I'm not hurt," Willoughby said, "but I may have lost control of my bladder functions. At least, I hope that's all it was. My leg's wet. What happened back there?"

"Hell, man, you was there. We got ambushed, that's what."

"Chiricahuas?"

Brubs shook his head. "Didn't see none of them, but they wasn't Cherry Cows. Had of been, we'd be dead now, or maybe just wishin' we was. Besides, whoever was back there had big-bore rifles. Couple of 'em Sharps Fifties, judgin' from the sound. Injuns don't have many big-bore guns. Had to be white men, maybe Mexican bandits." He glanced back over his shoulder. There was no sign of pursuit. "We best get to raisin' us some dust, Dave. They might come at us yet."

The two rode silently at a fast, bone-jarring trot for another mile, then Willoughby turned to Brubs. "Did you see our fearless gunfighter, Brazos?"

Brubs spat in disgust. "Wished I could of got off a shot at the little bastard. He didn't even pull a gun. Bet he's halfway back to San 'Tone by now."

"Maybe he went for help."

"Help, my butt," Brubs grumbled. "He went for help, all right — helpin' hisself keep from gettin' ventilated by a slug."

Willoughby sighed. "I can't say that I blame him all that much. So what do we do now?"

Brubs twisted in the saddle to stare along the back trail. "Nothin' much we can do. Can't help those men back there, and there ain't no chance of gettin' the wagons back. Might as well head on back to San 'Tone."

"I guess you're right. I'm not looking forward to facing Mr. Pettibone. He was rather emphatic about the need for success on this trip. The Greeks once had a policy of killing messengers who brought bad news."

Brubs spat again. His mouth felt like it was lined with rabbit fur. From the back end of the rabbit. "He's gonna be madder'n a wet cat, sure enough. But there wasn't nothin' we could do about it."

The two rode in silence for another mile before Brubs cocked a quizzical eyebrow at Willoughby. "I thought you damn Yankees could shoot."

"I was of the same impression about you Johnny Rebs," Willoughby said. "I don't recall your having distinguished yourself as a sharpshooter back there."

Brubs winced and shook his head. "Damn wonder either side won the war."

Brubs McCallan leaned back against his saddle and listened to his belly growl.

All their grub had been in the wagons. The wagons were probably on their way to Mexico by now, Brubs figured, and he and Willoughby were still a day's ride from San Antonio, in a dry camp and with only part of a canteen of water each.

Dave Willoughby sat cross-legged by the small

camp fire that Brubs had built more out of habit than hope of coffee or meat. Willoughby was running a bit of rag tied to a string through the bore of his Winchester. He hadn't said much in the last few hours.

Brubs stared at the sky overhead. The stars were bright now, but would be fading some when the full moon pushed over the eastern horizon. The wind had died at sunset, and now the only voices in the night were the distant cry of a coyote, the whisper of a hunting owl's wings overhead, and the soft ripping sounds as the horses grazed. The silence was beginning to get under Brubs's skin.

"Funny how them stars seem to make pictures," Brubs said. He pointed a finger toward a cluster in the northern sky. "Like that bunch up there."

Willoughby glanced up. "That's Ursa Minor, the Little Bear. Look closely and you can see that the stellar configuration takes on the shape of a bear."

Brubs squinted toward the stars. "Don't see no bear," he said. "Looks to me like a picture of a big, thick steak with a slab of apple pie and a dipper of corn squeezin's, served up by a chesty little yellow-haired gal."

Willoughby grimaced. "I would appreciate it, my friend, if you didn't find food, liquor, or women in everything you see." He stowed the cleaning patch and string, thumbed cartridges into the rifle, and racked a round into the chamber. "I had almost succeeded in ignoring the hunger pains in my belly —" He abruptly broke off the comment and came to his feet, rifle at his shoulder and pointed toward the edge of camp.

"What the hell's got into you?"

"I heard something out there," Willoughby said.

Brubs waved a hand. "You're gettin' powerful twitchy here lately, partner. Just a pack rat, most likely."

"What I heard was the clink of a curb chain. You ever hear of a pack rat wearing a bridle?"

THREE

"Hello, the camp!" The call from the darkness held a distinct Mexican accent.

Brubs thumbed back the hammer of his rifle as he scrambled to his feet. "Who's out there?" he yelled.

"Merely a lone traveler, seeking a camp for an evening meal."

"Ride in, mister," Brubs called, "but keep your hands where we can see 'em — and they better not be holdin' nothin' but bridle reins."

An indistinct blur moved in the starlight, then took shape as the horseman neared. He was a wiry man in a broad-brimmed sombrero, mounted on a nervous little sorrel of obvious Spanish blood and leading a bigger but equally boogery bay packhorse. He reined in at the edge of the light cast by the small fire and lifted fingertips to the big hat brim in greeting.

"My name is Ignacio Cruz, a vaquero bound from San Antonio for Nuevo Laredo, where I am told there is ranch work to be had."

Brubs lowered the hammer of his rifle. The man seemed to be telling the truth — or at least as close to the truth as a Mexican ever told. "If you're lookin' for grub," Brubs said, "you come to the wrong camp."

51

The Mexican gestured toward the pack animal. "I have some bacon, cornmeal, and coffee. The fare is meager, but I would be honored to share what little I have."

"Brubs," Dave Willoughby whispered, "we don't know that this man is alone. There could be a dozen others out there, just waiting for us to relax our guard."

Brubs flashed a quick grin at Willoughby. "I don't care if this man is Old Scratch hisself if he's got grub." He turned back to the vaquero. "Light and set, amigo."

Ignacio Cruz stepped from the saddle. "You are wise to be cautious." White teeth flashed as a smile creased the vaquero's dark face. "There are bandits about."

"No kiddin'," Brubs said with a wry half grin. "We'd never of guessed." He waved the Mexican closer to the fire.

Up close, Ignacio Cruz looked the part of a vaquero. His legs were bowed, big Chihuahua spurs on worn boots jangled as he walked, and the chaps he wore were slick from use on the inside of the thighs. His face carried the deep lines of sun and wind. The eyes were dark brown or black and seemed to hold a twinkle of amusement, as if he had just told himself a joke. He carried an ancient Remington cap-and-ball revolver in a holster high on his right hip and a thin-bladed knife in a belt sheath. The stock of a rifle showed beneath the stirrup of a heavy, scarred stock saddle with a horn the size of a man's hand. A long rawhide riata was tied to the saddle horn by a leather thong. He kept his weathered hands well clear of the weapons. Brubs felt an instinctive liking for the vaquero.

"Thank you for your hospitality, amigos," Cruz said. His voice was soft and lyrical, and like his eyes, hinted at some inner amusement. He nodded toward the fire. "*Con permiso,* I will get my cooking tools and supplies from my packs and prepare a small meal."

Brubs nodded. His belly rumbled aloud. He was liking this Mexican better all the time. Cruz strode to the nervous bay and rummaged in his packs.

Brubs glanced at Willoughby. The lean Yankee still held his rifle, the hammer at full cock. "Put up the long gun, partner," he said softly. "This man's all right."

"How can you be sure?"

" 'Cause if he wasn't, he'd of shot us both already," Brubs said. "Relax, amigo. You got to learn to trust people more."

Willoughby cast a sharp glance at Brubs. "I'm beginning to learn otherwise, with you as a tutor," he said. But he eased the hammer and lowered his rifle.

The vaquero was a top-hand trail cook. Brubs swiped the last bit of bacon grease from the skillet with a fragment of cornbread, popped the soppins into his mouth, and reached for the tin can that served as his and Dave's communal coffee cup. Brubs leaned back, patted his stomach, and grinned at Cruz. "Mighty fine grub, amigo. Don't remember ever tastin' better."

Cruz's lips lifted in a smile. "Hunger is the best of all spices," he said. "Do you wish more?"

Brubs reluctantly shook his head. "Don't want to eat all your groceries. Wouldn't be neighborly, leavin' you short with a long ride comin' up. You say you come from San 'Tone? What's the news from there?"

Cruz reached in a vest pocket for a tobacco sack and papers, offered the makings to Brubs and Willoughby, then expertly rolled a smoke after the two declined. "Much excitement in San Antonio this week." The vaquero fired his quirly with a twig from the fire. "The wagons of a wealthy merchant named Pettibone were taken by bandits only a few days ago."

Brubs cocked an eyebrow. "That a fact?"

"*Sí.* A young man called Brazos rides in like the wind, as if fleeing the devil himself, and tells Señor Pettibone of a big fight with *bandidos.* This Brazos says he killed three bandits himself in the fight —"

"That lyin' little son —"

"Brubs," Willoughby quickly broke in, "it isn't polite to interrupt a guest." The dark look he sent toward Brubs translated as, *Shut up, dammit.* He turned to Ignacio. "Please continue."

Cruz took a deep drag at his cigarette and let the smoke trickle from his nostrils. "This Brazos fellow says to Señor Pettibone that two gringos

54

joined the bandit gang. That these two were —
how do you say it? Ah, yes. 'In cahoots' with
the *bandidos*."

"That lyin' little son —"

"Brubs!"

"Sorry, Ignacio."

"*De nada.* Anyhow, Señor Pettibone flies into
a rage. He places a reward on the heads of these
two gringos. He will pay twenty-five dollars in
silver for each of them."

"How much?" Brubs's question was a squawk
of outrage.

"Brubs, you're interrupting again." Willoughby leveled the *shut-the-hell-up* look at Brubs
once more. "Please continue, Señor Cruz."

Ignacio Cruz lifted an eyebrow. "It is a small
sum, true enough, for two such dangerous des-
peradoes. But I have known men who would slit
the throats of their own mothers for less than
that amount." Cruz took a final drag of his
smoke and ground the butt beneath a boot heel.
He leveled a steady, knowing gaze at Willoughby. "If I were to personally meet these two
young gringos, I think perhaps I would tell them
not to return to San Antonio. Señor Pettibone
is *enojado mucho* — very angry."

"If we should run across them," Willoughby
said, his brow furrowed, "we will advise them
as you would, Señor Cruz. Perhaps they are innocent of the allegations."

The vaquero shrugged. "Perhaps. I would not
trust the young man Brazos to tell the truth in

a confessional with a priest. I think perhaps he exaggerates a bit."

"Where is this Brazos fellow now, amigo?" Brubs asked.

"Who knows? Señor Pettibone fired him on the spot and told him to leave San Antonio *muy pronto*. I think Brazos maybe take his advice." Cruz reached for the skillet. "If you wish no more food, I will clean the cooking tools and be on my way."

"Might as well stay the night, Ignacio," Brubs said. He ignored Willoughby's warning glance. "It's too dark to travel, anyway."

Cruz glanced at the eastern sky. "Soon the moon will rise and turn the night into day. I must hurry to Nuevo Laredo."

"None of my business, Ignacio, but why the rush?" Brubs asked.

Cruz half smiled at Brubs. "A bit of trouble back in San Antonio. Nothing of great importance. But one should never tempt fate." He stooped to scour the skillet with sand, rinsed the coffeepot, and stored the utensils in a pack.

Brubs realized for the first time that Ignacio Cruz had not unsaddled the twitchy little sorrel. In fact, he hadn't even loosened the cinch. That wasn't like an ordinary vaquero. They took better care of their horses than they did their women, for which Brubs was grateful. It meant it was easier to take a Mexican's woman than his horse. Ignacio Cruz, Brubs decided, was definitely on the run. He wondered what the "bit of trouble" might be, but didn't think it would be too smart to push the point.

The moon pushed over the horizon, heavy and full, as Ignacio Cruz touched his hat brim in a final salute and kneed the snorting little sorrel toward the west.

Brubs and Willoughby stood for a moment in silence and watched the vaquero ride away. Then Brubs snorted in disgust. "Twenty-five dollars! That damned old tightwad skinflint! I ain't never been so plumb through insulted in all my born days!"

Willoughby stroked his chin in thought and stared at Brubs. "I don't know," he said cautiously, "twenty-five dollars sounds like a lot of money at the moment."

Brubs's outrage slowly faded. "What you lookin' at me like that for, Dave?"

Willoughby's solemn expression finally cracked into a slight grin. "Just wondering how far I could get on twenty-five dollars."

Brubs feigned a gasp of wounded indignation. "Dave Willoughby, how could you even think such a thing, after all I've done for you?"

"Exactly my point, my friend." Willoughby reached out and clapped Brubs on the shoulder. "Now, let's take stock and see what we're going to do." He led the way back to the fire, where the tin can held the last of the coffee from Ignacio Cruz's pot.

The two squatted beside the dying embers. Willoughby wrapped his bandanna around the can, sipped at the brew, and handed the tin to Brubs. "We're broke, we have no food or supplies, and now we're fugitives with a price — albeit a small one — on our heads. Going back to face Lawrence T. Pettibone is out of the question now." He sighed. "Do you think we should follow Ignacio, maybe get a job on one of the ranches down south?"

Brubs's brows bunched in thought. "Nah. I punched cows before. Long on hard work and short on payday. I tell you for a fact, partner, the only thing dumber'n a cow is a cowboy." He finished the last of the coffee and tossed the fire-scorched tin can aside.

"Maybe the railroads are hiring."

"Railroads? You're slap out of your mind, Dave. Swingin' a spike maul twelve hours a day?" Brubs snorted in disgust. "Sweat's somethin' you work up with a woman. It's pure poison anyplace else. Think about makin' money, amigo. Don't think about work."

Willoughby sighed. "It appears," he said, "that we have no salable skills. I suppose I could get a job teaching school."

"School! Dave, you got to quit usin' them dirty words around me like that." Brubs visibly cringed. "Work. School. Two things I spend my whole life avoidin', and you go and bring 'em up again. Besides, school teachin's no job for a man. That's woman's work. I'll think of somethin' else on the way back from San 'Tone."

Willoughby nodded and sat in silence for a

moment, staring at the fire, lost in thought. Then his head snapped up as if he had been goosed. "Wait a minute! Did you say on the way *back* from San Antonio?"

Brubs grinned and flexed his shoulders. "That's what I said, right enough."

"Now, wait a minute! We are *not* going to San Antonio!" Willoughby stared in disbelief at Brubs. "In case it may have slipped your mind, there's a short-tempered old man there who would gleefully kill us both with his bare hands — not to mention the fact that we now have a price on our heads." He peered hard at Brubs. "You're only joking, right?"

Brubs leaned back against his bedroll, his hands folded beneath his head. "I been thinkin', Dave. About Callie."

Willoughby bounded to his feet and stared down at Brubs. "You can't be serious!"

"Never been seriouser in my life, partner," Brubs said wistfully. "When I look up at that there moon and think about Callie lyin' under it and the way she was lookin' at me back in San 'Tone, I just get plumb wobbly in the knees."

Willoughby sniffed and frowned at Brubs. "You're wobbly all right, but not in the knees. Between the ears is more like it. Forget it, Brubs."

"Aw, Dave, you got to learn to quit frettin' like an old mama duck all the time. Man, that Callie's somethin'."

"She's something, all right. Something that'll get you dead. Remember what her father said?

'Touch her and I'll kill you,' or words to that effect." Willoughby squared his shoulders. "This time you're not going to drag me into another mess. Your crusade to get me killed is over. Deal me out."

Brubs sighed. "Dave, partner, think about it this way. That Juanita's got her cap set for you, sure as rain. All you got to do is whisper in her ear and she'll have them skirts up before you can say 'please, ma'am.' Now, maybe she ain't as pretty as Callie, but aside from a little extra meat here and there and that little mustache, she ain't half bad-lookin'. Just might be worth the chance. Besides, there ain't nothin' goin' to go wrong. I got it all planned out."

Willoughby started pacing the campsite, his gaze flicking back and forth.

"What you doin', partner?"

"Looking for a beer bottle so I can knock some sense back into your empty head." He stopped pacing and glared at Brubs. "I'm not going back there, and that is absolutely, positively, and inviolately final."

Brubs McCallan pulled his horse to a stop in the stand of cottonwoods and pecan trees along the creek behind Lawrence T. Pettibone's home and wagon yard on the outskirts of San Antonio. He glanced at the sky. The full moon sat fat and bright orange just over the lip of the eastern horizon.

Brubs stepped from the saddle and handed his

reins to Dave Willoughby. "Tie these mounts up down by that thick underbrush and spread the bedrolls under that biggest cottonwood, partner. I'll fetch the women."

Willoughby sighed heavily and reached for the reins. "I never thought insanity was contagious," he mumbled.

Brubs worked his way to the window of the ground-floor corner bedroom, keeping in the cover of the inky shadows cast by the rising full moon. He felt his heart skip a couple of beats as he tapped softly on the glass.

There was no response. He tapped again, then a third time. Finally, the window slid open.

"Who's there?"

Brubs sighed in relief at the sound of Callie's voice.

"Brubs McCallan."

"What do you want?"

"You know what I want, Callie. Same thing you want. Meet me under that big cottonwood down on the creek. Bring Juanita — Dave's with me. And a bottle of whiskey. Some grub wouldn't hurt none neither, if you've got it."

There was a brief hesitation, then the husky voice whispered, "All right. Give us a few minutes."

Brubs McCallan lay relaxed and content on the bedroll spread beneath the cottonwood tree, the moonlight through the leaves dappling the body of the naked woman beside him.

Juanita snored softly, her head nestled against Brubs's shoulder. Moonlight dusted the sprinkling of dark hair across her upper lip.

"Hey, Dave," Brubs said softly, "you through with my woman yet?"

"So it would appear."

Willoughby sounded tired, Brubs thought. He eased his arm slowly from beneath Juanita's head, and on impulse leaned down to kiss her lightly on the forehead. Brubs didn't know how he'd wound up with Juanita instead of Callie, but he figured he'd gotten the best of the deal anyway. No way could Callie be as good as Juanita. "We best get a move on, while there's still moonlight for ridin'."

Brubs slipped into his clothes, heard Juanita's soft snore and Callie's murmur of contentment from the other side of the cottonwood tree. He peeked around the tree trunk. Callie stood on her tiptoes and kissed Willoughby, her arms around his neck. Willoughby was trying to hold the kiss and button his pants at the same time.

"Come on, Dave," Brubs said. "We got to ride."

Twenty minutes later, Brubs kneed his horse into a slow trot. He heard Willoughby's deep sigh of relief as the Pettibone compound dropped out of sight behind the rolling hills.

"Now, partner, wasn't that worth a little gamble?" Brubs asked with a grin.

"If we get away, yes," Willoughby said. "If we don't, no."

The two rode in silence for a mile before Brubs chuckled. "How'd you wind up with my woman, anyway?"

Willoughby shrugged, then yawned. "I have no idea. It just sort of happened, I guess. Are you angry about it?"

"Hell, no," Brubs said emphatically. "That Juanita's somethin' else. Them Mex women know tricks no white girl ever thought of. Near made my heart quit a couple times. Damn that was some kinda fun. You bring the possibles sack?"

"The what?"

"Grub bag."

"Oh. Yes, I have it. Callie said there was coffee, flour, bacon, some sugar, salt, and some jerked beef in the sack. Along with a small skillet, coffeepot, and eating utensils."

"No whiskey?"

"No. I think we emptied the only bottle she brought."

Brubs shrugged. "Don't matter. We still got near everythin' a man needs to live in Texas anyhow. Somethin' for the belly and buttery knees for the soul. It don't get much better'n this, my Yankee friend. All we need now is some cash money to jingle in our pockets."

Willoughby yawned again. "I have thirty dollars."

Brubs glanced at Willoughby, surprised. "Where in the blue-eyed hell did you get thirty dollars?"

"Callie gave it to me."

Brubs frowned. "I didn't ask her to bring no money. Wonder why she done that?"

Willoughby shrugged. "I don't know. Maybe I did something she liked."

The sun was almost overhead before Brubs called a halt to rest the horses beside a small spring at the side of a shallow creek lined by knee-deep green grass.

It had been easy going throughout the night. They had left the main trail a few miles out of town, but the countryside had stood out plainly in the bright moonlight. The sun came up in a clear, bright sky. Brubs figured they were better than thirty miles from San Antonio. Far enough away from old man Pettibone to catch a little rest, anyway.

The two riders topped their canteens from the spring and let the horses drink. Brubs loosened the cinch to let the sorrel blow. "Might as well squat a spell, Dave. Break out that coffeepot. I sure could use a cup."

Dave Willoughby let the cinches on his black out a couple notches, then rummaged in the possibles sack. Brubs had a small fire going within minutes. Willoughby hobbled the horses to graze in the lush grass beside the spring as the water for the coffee heated. Brubs squatted on his heels beside the fire, the sun hot on his back. It would be a scorcher by mid-afternoon.

Willoughby wandered back and sat beside Brubs.

"By the by," Brubs said, "I found out about Ignacio Cruz. Juanita told me."

"Juanita knows him?"

"Cousins. Hell, all Mexes are cousins, amigo. Even if they don't stay married to each other." Brubs grinned. "Seems like this 'little trouble' Ignacio mentioned wasn't so little after all. He killed two men in a gunfight down in a south San 'Tone cantina. Wasn't his first, neither."

"What? That man was a killer?"

Brubs nodded. "Knowed it right off. You notice how slick-worn the grips of that old cap-and-ball pistol was? I seen it in his eyes, too. Killer's eyes. Kinda cold-like. Juanita says he's shot seven, eight men, not countin' Injuns. Reward out on 'im. Five hundred dollars."

Willoughby's eyes went wide. "Do you mean to tell me that I shared a camp with a cold-blooded killer? A gunfighter?"

Brubs chuckled. "Mexes ain't cold-blooded. Downright hotbloods, in fact. Juanita was, for sure. Anyhow, I figgered there was a price on old Ignacio's head. Didn't know how much at the time, but by my cipherin' even five hundred ain't enough to try and throw down on that jasper."

Willoughby cast a quick glance toward the sky. "God, I don't believe this. I left a comfortable bed and a family of means back East to find adventure and make my name in Texas. And so

65

far I've been in a saloon brawl, been shot at, rubbed elbows with a gunfighter, took a chance on getting skinned alive by a raging father, and I've got a price on my head. And that's just since I met you, Brubs McCallan."

"Yep," Brubs said. "Stick with me, partner, and I'll make a Texan out of you yet. Which reminds me, I got a present for you."

"A what?"

Brubs strode to his horse, untied a long rawhide riata from a near side thong, and carried it back to the fire. He tossed the riata to Willoughby. "Noticed you didn't have a rope, so I swiped one for you."

"Swiped one?"

"Yeah. Took it out of one of old man Pettibone's wagons."

Willoughby groaned. "You *stole* from Lawrence T. Pettibone?"

Brubs shrugged. "Figgered it wouldn't hurt none. He was mad at us anyhow. Besides, that's likely the rope he'd of hung us with if he'd caught us."

Willoughby's shoulders slumped. "Add theft to my list of sins. What do I need this for?"

"That riata's one of the things that'll make us rich men, amigo."

A puzzled look came over Willoughby's face. "I don't know what you're driving at, Brubs, but I can't use a lariat."

"You what?" Mock disbelief sounded in Brubs's tone. "You can't use a rope? Why, son, when you was studyin' at that highfalutin college, I was studyin' ropin'. Now we'll see which studyin' pays best out here." He shook his head and chuckled. "We had some of the wildest chickens man ever saw. I'll learn you how to use a rope, Dave. Can't make a real genuine Texan out of you if you can't throw a decent loop."

"If I live that long," Willoughby said wistfully. "So what's this got to do with our becoming wealthy?"

Brubs plucked a long stem of grass and stuck it between his teeth. "Horses."

"Come again?"

"Remember those mustangs we passed on the way out with old Pettibone's wagons?"

Willoughby leaned forward, rummaged in the possibles sack, and dumped a handful of coffee into the pot. "Of course I remember," he said. "It's hard to forget such a sight."

Brubs bit into the grass stem. The flavor was sharp and bittersweet. "I seen a dust cloud an hour ago. Had to be mustangs on the move out yonder, not more'n a couple days' ride off. And you remember John Blue said they don't belong to nobody?"

The coffeepot started blurping. "Why don't you just come straight to the point, Brubs? I get nervous when you talk in a circle." Willoughby added a dollop of cold water to settle the grounds, then pulled a pair of tin cups from the possibles sack.

"We're going to catch 'em."

"What?"

"Catch us a bunch of them horses." Brubs heard the growing excitement in his own voice. "We can sell 'em for ten, maybe fifteen dollars a head. More if they're broke to saddle or good breedin' mares." He chuckled aloud. "Amigo, we're goin' to be *mesteñeros* — mustangers. There's thousands of dollars out there, just waitin' for us." He clapped Dave playfully on the shoulder. "It'll be just like pickin' money off a tree."

The worry lines in Willoughby's brow deepened as he poured the coffee. "Where would we sell these horses? Provided, of course, that we can catch them in the first place."

Brubs sipped at the brew and winced. The tin rim of the cup was hotter than the coffee it held. "That sure ain't no problem. Ever' rancher in north and east Texas and up into Kansas and Arkansas needs horses. They're up to their butts in cattle, but good horses is hard to find. We just catch a few, trail 'em to a buyer, and ride off with silver jinglin' in our pockets."

Willoughby took a sip of his coffee, his forehead still furrowed. "If it's that easy to catch these wild horses, why isn't everyone else doing it?"

Brubs said, "A few of 'em are, I reckon. Mexes and Injuns, mostly. But they just chousin' a few at a time. They ain't thinkin' big, whole herds, like we are." He lifted his cup in a toast.

"Here's to shiny gold, wild women, and good whiskey in our future, partner."

Willoughby hesitated. "I don't know about this, Brubs. It sounds to me like it could be hard and dangerous work."

"Dave, you are the most down-in-the-mouth feller I ever met," Brubs chided. "Always lookin' for boogers."

Willoughby sighed. "One of us has to be realistic about this. I don't know the first thing about catching mustangs. I suppose you're an expert on the subject?"

Brubs downed the last of his coffee and said, "No, I ain't no expert. But we got us good, fast horses. Now we both got good ropes. Besides, what could be so hard about catchin' wild horses? You just chase 'em down, rope 'em, and sell 'em."

Willoughby dropped his gaze to the riata at his feet. "Brubs, every time you say something will be easy, I get this fluttery sensation in my belly."

"You got any other ideas?"

Willoughby sighed heavily. "We could start robbing banks."

Brubs lifted both eyebrows. "Now, Dave, get serious. You know a man could get hurt doin' that."

"Riding with you, Brubs McCallan," Willoughby said solemnly, "a man could get hurt going to a Baptist camp meeting."

FOUR

Dave Willoughby eased his long-legged black around the clump of mesquite at the lip of a broad valley studded with brush, rocks, and prickly pear, and felt his breath catch in his throat.

The iron-gray mustang stallion stood a hundred yards away on the valley floor, head held high, nostrils flared and testing the wind, its long black mane and tail whipped by the stiff breeze. Another twenty yards back a band of a dozen mares stood patiently, watching the stallion. Two of the mares were heavy with foals. Several weanling colts played at the edge of the herd, bucking, squealing, and nipping at each other.

Willoughby felt his heart pound against his ribs and the anxious quiver of the black's muscles between his knees. He sat transfixed for a moment, awed by his first close look at the wild horses that gave Mustang Desert its name. The mustangs weren't especially pretty. The small, wiry animals would never take any ribbons at the Cincinnati Equestrian Society's annual benefit horse show. Yet, there was something about them, a shaggy wild magnificence that conveyed a sense of dignity.

Willoughby finally shook away the feeling of

near disbelief. He glanced over his shoulder and motioned to the stocky rider on the big sorrel, then pointed toward the valley floor. Brubs McCallan kneed his horse alongside and glanced at the stallion and his band of mares below.

"Hot damn, Dave, we're in business," Brubs said excitedly. He whipped the tie thong from his hemp rope and shook out a loop. "Let's go get us some horses." He drove spurs to the sorrel and let loose a whoop of exuberance as the gelding charged down the rocky slope. Willoughby's black bolted after Brubs's sorrel, eager to take up the chase.

The mustang stud wheeled with a squeal and a shake of the head, tossing its long forelock. Almost as one the mares spun on their heels and were in a dead run within two strides, hooves kicking dust and gravel, tails flying straight out behind them. Willoughby's heart leapt in his throat as his black stumbled and almost went down; the gelding regained its feet and plowed between two mesquites. Willoughby barely had time to throw a forearm in front of his face before the thorny branches tore at his arms and legs.

Brubs's sorrel was two strides in front when a hoof ripped a prickly pear from the valley floor and tossed it in the air. The cactus pad spun high, descended, and drove its needle-sharp spines deep into Willoughby's upper thigh. His yelp of pain was drowned in the thunder of hooves as the mustangs pounded across the valley and jumped a shallow dry wash. Dave's eyes teared from the wind and dust until he could see only vague, blurred shapes.

The mustangs had gained a hundred yards on the pursuers by the time the wild band charged up the far slope of the valley and stretched into a flat-out run across the brushy flats beyond. Willoughby almost lost his seat in the saddle as his black hurdled the creek and landed with a bone-rattling thump on the far side. The impact tossed Willoughby forward in the saddle. His thigh slammed into the pommel with the prickly pear between skin and leather. He gritted his teeth against the fiery pain in his leg and settled in for the chase.

The run lasted a little over two miles. The mustangs had gained a quarter of a mile on the pursuers before Brubs eased his lathered sorrel to a stop. It took Willoughby a few yards further to stop the willing but winded black. He felt the horse's ribs heaving for air between his legs as Brubs trotted up alongside.

Willoughby wiped a bloody, thorn-scratched hand across his watery eyes and glared at Brubs. "I thought you said this would be easy," he grumbled.

Brubs ignored him. "Damn, those mustangs can run somewhat," he said, re-coiling his loop. "Made this racehoss sorrel of mine look like he was goin' backwards. But it don't matter. We'll get the next bunch. There's plenty of wild horses around here."

"So why did it take us two days to find this herd?" Willoughby eased a cautious finger under the prickly pear pad and tugged. His breath whistled between his teeth at the sharp stab of pain in the pierced flesh.

Brubs flashed a quick grin. "There you go again with that down-in-the-mouth stuff." He eyed Willoughby from hat crown to boot heel. "Amigo, you look like hell. Ain't you figgered out yet you're supposed to ride *around* them mesquites and catclaws?"

"Tell that to this fool black horse," Willoughby said. He stared at the prickly pear pad buried deep in his leg, at the scratches and cuts on his arms, at the tattered remnants of what had been a good shirt only minutes ago.

Brubs ran a quick glance over the black gelding. "No problem, partner," he said. "Your horse didn't get hurt."

Willoughby leveled a chilly glare at Brubs. "Now that," he said, "is truly a comfort. Do you think you might be able to help remove this cactus from my leg? It stings a bit."

Brubs swung from the saddle, walked to Willoughby's side, slipped a thumb and finger under the pear pad, and yanked.

Willoughby yelped aloud as the barbed spines ripped through his flesh. Blood from the punctures welled through the cloth of his pants leg. He ground his teeth and waited for the pain to ease. It didn't. "Thanks, Doctor Death," he said when he could speak again.

"Glad to help," Brubs said. "Likely some of them thorns broke off in your leg. We get back to camp, I'll dig 'em out for you."

Willoughby raised a hand. "If you don't mind, I'll do that myself. Your bedside manner leaves something to be desired. By the way, how far is it back to camp?"

Brubs shrugged. "Not more'n eleven, twelve miles." His face brightened under the bushy handlebar mustache and he scratched the tousled, sweat-darkened sandy hair that curled about his neck. "Maybe we'll jump another bunch on the way back."

"We won't," Willoughby said, "if there's a God in heaven."

Brubs's brow wrinkled. "Yeah, I reckon you're right, partner. Our horses is plumb wore out."

Dave Willoughby winced as he eased the point of his pocketknife under a festering thorn, gripped the back side of the spine with his thumb, and yanked the barbed needle from his leg. He held the thorn up to the light of the camp fire and studied it for a moment. "I thought I had all of these things dug out four days ago," he said.

Brubs McCallan glanced at the thorn and shrugged. "No way to get 'em all out. They got little barbs on 'em like fishhooks. Devil's own time to pull 'em loose." He added reassuringly, "Don't fret it none, though. They'll work their way through and come out on the other side someday. If they don't hit a bone or nerve on the way through."

Willoughby said dryly, "It never ceases to amaze me how much comfort you bring a man." He tossed the thorn into the small fire and pulled up his pants, then leaned back against his bedroll and stared at the sky above. The heavens were ablaze with stars, a blanket against the near blackness overhead. After a moment, he sighed. "Well, at least I've accomplished one objective."

Brubs refilled a tin cup from the coffeepot and handed it to Dave. "What's that, partner?"

"I wanted to get away from the city crowds, the mobs of people always pushing and shoving and in a hurry to get somewhere. It appears that I have managed to do that."

"Yeah," Brubs said, "I reckon you got that part of it right." He leaned back against his saddle. "Downright nice and peaceful out here, sure enough. Makes a man want to put some of it in a bottle and save it for later, when he's got to feelin' pushed and crowded and sorry for hisself and needs a pick-me-up."

Willoughby was silent for a moment. "I never thought of it that way, but you do raise a good point."

"Dave?"

"Yes?"

"It ain't really none of my business, but I got my curious up. Want to tell me how come you left home and what you left behind?"

Willoughby sighed again. "It's a long story."

"I ain't goin' nowhere. Not till daylight, any-how."

Willoughby slipped a hand beneath his but-tocks, removed a small rock, and tossed it aside. "My family is rather prominent back East. Mer-cantile business, banking, politics and the like. Quite wealthy, really." He paused for a sip from his coffee cup. "I never saw much of Father. He was always busy with something or other. And Jules, my older brother, and I never got along all that well."

"Family spat?"

"You might say that. They wanted me to take over the family businesses someday, maybe run for the Senate. They couldn't understand that I was not interested in spending my life that way. They even picked out a girl for me. A good match of bloodlines and money, they said. I didn't like her. It made all of them quite angry when I said no."

"That when the fight started?"

Willoughby reached out, plucked a twig from a nearby mesquite, and tucked it in the corner of his mouth. "Not really. It's hard to say when the disputes began. They seemed to have been going on all my life. Anyway, to abbreviate the story, the war came along while I was in college. Father paid another man to take my place so I wouldn't have to go fight, without asking me first. I guess that was the proverbial straw that broke the camel's back." He worried a sliver of jerky from between his teeth and spat. "By then,

I was more than a little tired of the family making all my decisions for me. I left home, enlisted, lived through the war, and just never went back."

"How come you picked Texas?"

Willoughby tongued the twig for a moment, then shrugged. "I had read and heard a lot about Texas. It sounded like a place where a man could make his own life, instead of having everything forced on him." He cocked an eyebrow at Brubs. "Your turn. Tell me something about Brubs McCallan."

Brubs sipped at his coffee and stared for a moment into the dying embers of the fire. "Not all that much to tell. Never knew my pa and not much more'n that about Ma."

"What happened? Disease or something take them?"

"Nope. I just never knew 'em. Ma was a whore over in Nacogdoches. She didn't know who my pa was. I was just a baby when she give me to a farm couple outside of town for raisin'. I never heard anything about her after that."

Willoughby frowned. "That must have been difficult for you. As a child, I mean. Didn't you hate them — your folks — for abandoning you like that?"

Brubs chuckled. "Hell, no. If Ma hadn't been a whore and Pa hadn't had an itch for her to scratch, I wouldn't be here now. I figger Pa had to be a cowman, 'cause I never been known for any special smarts." The grin faded. "No, I don't hate 'em. Wonder about 'em sometimes, but I never fretted much about bein' a bastard. Always figgered it beat hell out of not bein' born t'all." He sighed. "I do miss the folks who took me in. They were good people. Both of 'em died just before the war. I didn't have no other family, no other place to go, and I'd had all the farmin' I needed to last me a lifetime. So I wound up with Hood."

Willoughby was silent for a moment. He finished his coffee, then said, "Do you still think the Confederacy was right?"

Brubs shrugged. "I was too young then to know nothin'. Now I'm older and still don't know nothin'. Anyhow, it didn't take me long to figger out a man could sure as hell get killed. Still don't know what side was right. I ain't no educated college boy like one hoss chaser I know."

Willoughby said, "The same problem in ethics bothered me, too. I finally decided the whole mess wasn't about slavery or freedom or any of those noble topics the legislators and newspapers ranted about. The whole thing was about economics and politics and power. The people who really won were those who owned companies that made guns and gunpowder."

Brubs rose, rinsed the two tin cups, and stored them with the remaining handful of camp supplies. He said, "By God, we'd of whipped you bluecoats if we coulda made a catapult big enough to throw cotton bales at you. That's about all we had to fight with."

Willoughby crawled from atop his bedroll, spread the blankets, and started pulling off his boots. "The only good thing about that war is that it's over." He settled back and stared at the sky for a long time.

In the near distance a coyote yipped three times, then loosed a long, mournful wail. Brubs reached for his rifle, then relaxed as the coyote cry faded. Its voice cracked on the final note.

"What's the matter?" Willoughby asked, sitting up in alarm.

"Nothin'. There for a minute I thought it might have been Cherry Cows or Comanches," Brubs said. "Most Injuns use critter calls to talk with when they're bein' sneaky. But no self-respectin' Injun would howl like that. Nothin' but a natural coyote hits them kind of sour notes."

Brubs settled into his blankets, removing only his hat, boots, and pistol belt for the night.

"Brubs?"

"Still here."

"We've run three bunches of mustangs and have never even gotten close enough to throw a rope. We're as far from being rich now as we were back in the San Antonio jail, and running low on supplies to boot. Aren't you getting a bit discouraged?"

"No, partner," Brubs said. "Matter of fact, I've had a bunch of fun runnin' them horses. It's like women. The chousin's near as much fun as the catchin' sometimes. Besides, we'll get us at least one tomorrow." His tone was confident.

"How do you know that?"

"Got it all figgered out, amigo. You just watch old Brubs McCallan and I'll show you how to catch a mustang."

Dave Willoughby sprawled on his belly on the ridge overlooking the valley where they had jumped the iron-gray mustang's band a few days before.

The sun was barely a couple of hand spans above the eastern horizon, but already heat waves danced across the plain below. There was no sign of movement in the valley. He glanced at Brubs, who also lay on his stomach, the forestock of the old .44 rimfire rifle resting across a folded blanket.

"How do you know they'll come today?"

Brubs's mustache twitched in a slight grin. "You read the sign, amigo. This bunch waters ever' mornin' at that little spring down there. They'll be around."

Willoughby shifted his gaze back to the valley and fought against the edgy feeling in his gut. "Are you sure this will work?"

Brubs patted the scarred stock of the rifle. "It'll work. Just takes a man can shoot straight."

Willoughby sighed. He wasn't convinced. Brubs had said he had heard about the "creasing" technique from an old mustanger up in the Pease River country.

As Brubs described it, the hunter set up a shooting stand, waited for the horses to come by, picked out the one he wanted, and then shot the animal. The slug had to nick the mustang's neck just enough to jolt the bones and shock the spinal cord; that would stun the animal and knock it down. Then, before it could recover, the hunter rushed in to put ropes on the horse. It seemed chancy to Dave. Brubs's old beat-up rifle didn't look to be that accurate, and seventy yards was pushing the effective range of a .44 rimfire load. A neckbone or tailbone was a small enough target at ten yards, let alone seventy. Willoughby squirmed on the sandy, pebbled ground. The rawhide riata in his hand was already beginning to turn slick from sweat.

"Be still, partner," Brubs muttered softly. "Man's huntin', he's got to be quiet and almighty patient. Them mustangs'll be along any minute now. You just be ready with that rope."

The sun had moved halfway up the eastern sky before Brubs said softly, "Here they come." He settled the brass plate of the rifle butt against his shoulder.

Willoughby watched as the mustang band slowly made its way down the far slope into the valley. The iron-gray stallion had the lead, alert and wary. The gray stopped every few feet to stand, head lifted high and nostrils flared, as it looked around and sniffed the air for danger. Willoughby held his breath as the stud seemed to look straight at him. Then the gray dropped its head and moved forward a few more yards. The mares and colts followed cautiously, watching the stallion for any warning signs.

The stallion trotted past the cactus bush Brubs had chosen as a range finder. Moments later a handsome sorrel mare, bigger and more muscled than the others of the band, neared the cactus range marker. Willoughby knew from experience that the sorrel was the strongest and fastest mare in the band. The yearling colt at her side was a good one. She would make someone a fine broodmare.

"Okay, honey," Brubs whispered. "Come to Papa."

The crack of Brubs's rifle hammered against Willoughby's ears. Through the billow of powder smoke, Dave saw the sorrel mare drop in her tracks. The rest of the band wheeled and bolted. The downed mare's hooves cribbed at the sand of the valley floor.

"Let's go get her, Dave," Brubs shouted. "Get the ropes on her before she comes to."

Willoughby sprinted to the downed mare, his rawhide riata in hand with Brubs a couple of yards behind. He skidded to a stop, winded, slipped a loop over a front foot, then abruptly straightened to stare down at the sorrel mare.

"Wrap up that other front foot quick," Brubs said, puffing for air as he stumbled to a stop alongside.

"No need." Willoughby's voice was soft.

"What do you mean, no need? Move, man! She'll be coming to any minute now."

"No she won't."

"What?"

"She's dead, Brubs." Willoughby stared at the small, bloody hole a hand span beneath the mare's flowing mane. "Your shot went low. Broke her neck."

Brubs leaned over the mare. "Well, I'll be damned," he said incredulously. "Wonder how that happened? She must of moved just as I touched the shot off."

Willoughby cast a disgusted glance at his partner. "No, she didn't. You just flat-out missed."

Brubs stared at the rifle in his hands for a moment. "Must of been a bad cartridge." Then he shrugged and turned to Dave with a grin. "Didn't work out all bad."

"You kill a good mare as dead as last year's grass," Willoughby said, shaking his head in dismay, "and then say it wasn't all bad? How do you figure that?"

Brubs said casually, "Well, amigo, we've got fresh meat for supper."

Willoughby stepped back and stared in disbelief at his saddle partner. "*Horse* meat?"

Brubs shucked his skinning knife from its belt sheath and tested the edge with a thumb. "Don't go gettin' all picky till you try it, partner," he said. "Horse meat ain't half bad. 'Specially if you're as tired of jackrabbit and jerky as I am." He knelt over the dead mare. "Course, mule meat's a lot better. Comanche'd kill you quicker for a good, fat mule than they would for your scalp. Grab your knife and lend a hand. We got to butcher out the best eatin' parts before the blowflies get too bad."

Willoughby sighed and reached for his knife, wondering why he couldn't seem to stay mad at Brubs McCallan for more than a couple of minutes. "I guess you're right," he grumbled. "It could have been worse."

"Glad to hear you say that," Brubs said. "Sounded like you was gettin' a little testy there for a spell."

"It could have been worse. With your talent for marksmanship, you could have shot me instead of the horse." Willoughby picked up a foreleg, knife poised, and glanced at Brubs. "If the rest of the Johnny Rebs shot like you do, it's a wonder the war lasted as long as it did."

Dave Willoughby sat cross-legged beside the camp fire and worried a piece of broiled mare meat from between his teeth with a mesquite thorn. He hated to admit it, but horse meat really wasn't all that bad. A little tougher than prime yearling steer beef, perhaps, but considerably better than what they had been eating, which was close to nothing.

Brubs McCallan heaved a sigh of contentment and patted his belly. "All I need now to be a happy man," he said, "is a bottle of whiskey and a willin' woman."

Willoughby cocked an eyebrow. "McCallan, do you ever think of anything except whiskey and women?"

"Not if I can help it. Thinkin' about anything else makes my head hurt. How much coffee we got left?"

Willoughby rummaged in the possibles sack, then shook his head. "Maybe enough for four or five days, if we ration ourselves to one cup in the morning. We're just about out of flour, salt, and sugar, too."

"How much of that thirty dollars we got left?"

Willoughby dug into his pockets and poked through a handful of coins and crumpled bills. "Fourteen dollars. Fitting out for this little expedition was expensive. Are you thinking about popping down to the corner grocer's shop for supplies?"

"Might as well, in a few days," Brubs said. "Got to be one somewhere within fifty, sixty miles of here."

Willoughby stuffed the money back in his pocket. "Which brings up the question," he said, "of where, exactly, is *here?*"

"Out under the Creator's fine sky, amigo, with not a worry in the world," Brubs said with a wide grin. "I figure we're somewhere northwest of Laredo. We'll catch us some mustangs in a couple days, then take us a little shoppin' trip." He belched. "Laredo's got some mighty fine-lookin' señoritas."

Willoughby sighed. "I hate to throw water on

your camp fire, but in case you haven't noticed, we have not exactly been setting the world ablaze as mustangers. We've been out in this desert long enough to count as forever, and all we have to show for our efforts are saddle scald, thorn punctures, and brush scars."

Brubs pried a sliver of mare steak from behind an eyetooth with a fingernail, spat, and grinned. "Been turnin' that over in my head. I got a new plan."

Willoughby loosed a low moan. "Every new plan you come up with seems to cost me a strip or two of skin. What's on your mind now — besides women and whiskey?"

"We been goin' at it wrong."

"No kidding?" The sarcasm was heavy in Willoughby's tone. Brubs didn't seem to notice.

"Sure 'nuff. First thing we got to do is find us some new country. This bunch we been chousin's got plumb boogery on us. First light tomorrow, we'll move fifty, sixty miles west. Ought to be some good mustang country over there." Brubs's words held a growing excitement. "We'll find us a new bunch, then do things different. I been thinkin'."

Willoughby sighed. *"Quad di omen avertant."*

Brubs cut a quick glance at Dave. "Talk American."

"It translates as, 'May the gods avert this omen.' I have this feeling an ancient Roman philosopher named Cicero must have ridden with one of your ancestors."

86

Brubs's thick brows bunched. "You mean they had mustangs way back then?"

"Possibly. Wild horses do make philosophers, that's for certain. So, what's this latest flash of inspiration?"

"We quit tryin' to chouse 'em down from behind. That ain't workin'. So," Brubs added confidently, "what we do is we catch a bunch on the flats or in a valley, but we split up — you come at 'em from one side, I come at 'em from the other. Get 'em between us and we can rope a couple while they're tryin' to figure out which way to run."

Willoughby was silent for a moment, staring at the darkening sky overhead.

"Well, partner? What do you think?" Brubs said.

"I'm thinking," Willoughby said, "that I had better get down to some serious worrying about the state of my own sanity."

"Why's that?"

"You're beginning to make sense."

Dave Willoughby felt a quiver of excitement as the mustangs grazed their way into the meadow.

There were at least forty wild horses in view now, two groups separated by perhaps a hundred yards, each under the command of a stallion. And for once, the terrain favored the mustangers.

The meadow was mostly open and relatively

flat, a few cottonwood and elm trees along a shallow creek the only obstructions to a chase beyond the usual mesquite clumps and cactus patches. Willoughby kept a tight rein on the eager black between his knees, holding the animal deep into the shadows at the edge of a mesquite thicket on the west side of the meadow. Brubs waited across the way, his sorrel tucked back behind a rockfall. A few more yards and the wild horses would be easing into the trap.

Willoughby held the rawhide riata in a sweaty palm, a loop already shaken out and the free end tied fast to the saddle horn. The seemingly endless practice sessions with the riata were about to pay off; Dave felt the eagerness that Brubs had described as "rope crazy" stir in his gut.

The first band of mustangs, led by an unusually tall and heavily muscled chestnut stallion, its hide covered with scars and part of an ear missing, were almost between Willoughby and Brubs now. The mares moved slowly, cropping at the clumps of grass along the creek. The chestnut's head snapped up, nostrils flared. The stallion stared toward the rockfall where Brubs waited. Its muzzle moved up and down as it tested the wind.

"Now, Brubs," Willoughby whispered aloud, "they're about to bolt —" A whoop from the far side of the meadow cut short Dave's soft comment. The sorrel charged from the rockfall, ears back, Brubs already swinging a big loop.

The chestnut stallion squealed, spun on its haunches, and charged toward the closest mare. The mustangs wheeled away from Brubs, thundering straight toward Willoughby. He touched spurs to the black's ribs.

The mustangs were barely twenty yards away when Willoughby's mount bolted from the mesquites. The horses wheeled, trying to escape the new threat, but Dave's black gained another ten yards before the mustangs were able to line out. Willoughby leaned low over the black's neck, spurring the gelding to more speed, and felt his spirits soar as a paint mare began to fall behind the main herd. The black closed the gap to five yards, then three. Willoughby whirled his riata overhead twice and cast the loop.

He whooped in joy as the loop dropped over the mare's head — but, in his excitement, forgot to jerk the slack. The rawhide rope settled deep around the mare's neck, almost halfway down her chest. Willoughby's yell of triumph ended in a startled squawk. In the heat of the chase he hadn't noticed the cottonwood tree.

Willoughby's black noticed it; he ducked to the left, missing the trunk of the tree by three feet. The paint mare went to the right, trailing a good thirty feet of rawhide rope. Willoughby barely had time to bark a curse when the jolt of the mare's weight against the riata staggered the black; the shock jerked the mare around into a circular turn. She went past the tree to the outside of Willoughby's black. The taut riata swept the front legs out from under Dave's horse as the mare ran past. Willoughby flipped over the falling black's ears, hit the ground hard on his back, skidded through a catclaw bush, and rolled in a cloud of dust. White lights flashed in his head as a stone cracked against his skull a split second before a fallen tree limb thumped into his ribs.

Willoughby wound up on his side, looking back at his horse. The black's hooves and head flailed as the horse tried to regain its feet. A sharp crack sounded as the riata parted. The paint mare whirled and ran toward the band of mustangs disappearing into the distance behind a dust cloud. The black finally scrambled to its feet and stood, hide trembling and nostrils flared.

Willoughby tried to pull air back into his lungs. They weren't working. He almost blacked out from lack of breath before he finally managed a quick gasp. He lay stunned, unable to move a muscle. He heard hoofbeats approaching on the run and steeled himself to be trampled to death.

"Partner? You all right?"

Willoughby somehow found the strength to turn his head and look up. Brubs McCallan still sat in the saddle, his hemp lariat rope in hand and a worried frown on his face. "You hurt?"

"Fool question," Willoughby managed to gasp.

Brubs dismounted and knelt at Dave's side. "Bust anything in that wreck?"

"Don't . . . think so." As Willoughby began to get more wind back, the pain started. His head hurt, his ribs ached, and raw patches where skin had once been felt burned by the fires of hell. He finally managed to sit up.

"Partner, I got to talk to you about your ropin' style," Brubs said. "You're supposed to keep both horses on the same side of the tree."

"You . . . are truly a pure comfort . . . to a dying man," Willoughby gasped. The landscape blurred, then tilted first one way and then the other. He shook his head to clear his vision. It just made the pain worse.

Brubs McCallan chuckled. "Boy, that was some kinda wreck, sure enough. Couldn't see nothin' but horse hocks, elbows, and hineys there for a while. Why, I'd of paid good money to watch that —"

"Brubs, shut up."

"Your horse looks okay. The honda busted on that riata of yours. I'll tie you up another one. Why, we won't miss a lick. Reckon you can stand up?"

"Don't know that I want to," Willoughby said. He felt a trickle down his cheek, swiped at it with a scraped hand, and stared for a moment at the smear of blood. A canteen appeared under his nose. Willoughby twisted the cap off with a bruised hand and took a swallow. The water stayed down. He lifted an eyebrow at Brubs. "I guess you . . . got one . . . roped and tied down?"

Brubs shook his head in bewilderment. "Damnedest thing. I never missed a good loop that clean before."

"So I go through . . . all this . . . and we have nothing to show for it?"

Brubs chuckled. "You got some right valuable schoolin'. Learned a lot about ropin' wild horses here today. I'll fetch your black. We'll try 'em again tomorrow."

"We will not," Willoughby grumbled. "I've left pieces of skin over half this desert. I've got thorns stuck in places I didn't even know I had. I've got a headache, my ribs may be cracked, and I'm hurting all over." He struggled to his feet and stood, wavering slightly. "Bring me my horse. I'm going back to that San Antonio jail before you manage to get me killed."

Brubs laughed aloud. "Aw hell, partner, we done been through the worst of it. It can't do nothin' but get better now."

A booming voice from close by jolted both men. "Just what in the blue-eyed hell do you two jackasses think you're doing?"

Willoughby turned. The man on the big roan horse seemed to have materialized from nowhere. He sat in the saddle beside a gnarled cottonwood. His face was deeply lined, weathered almost the color of harness leather, and sprouted a wiry and wild gray beard. He was short, but an ax handle wide, and his eyes were steely gray.

The most impressive thing about him was the rifle.

It was a Sharps Fifty. Its bore looked as big as a badger hole.

And the muzzle was trained squarely on Willoughby's shirtfront.

FIVE

"Don't either of you damn fools so much as twitch an eyeball," the man on the roan said, "on account of I'm just looking for an excuse to drop a hammer on you right now."

Brubs McCallan raised a hand. "If you're lookin' for somebody to rob, mister, you done picked the wrong bank."

"Rob, hell." The steel-gray eyes narrowed to bare slits. "I've been working that bunch of mustangs for four days, and you two idiots just boogered them into the next state. That's why I'm thinking serious-like about killing the both of you."

"Sure would appreciate it if you didn't," Brubs said. "That would certain spoil a passin' good day."

The old-timer glared at Brubs for a few heartbeats, as if trying to decide whether shooting the two would be worth the effort. "What are you boneheaded whelps doing out here besides giving me a bellyache?"

"Mustangin'," Brubs said.

The man on the roan snorted in disgust. "I've been watching you two most of a day now. If what you're doing is mustanging, I'm a Methodist preacher." He shifted a cud of tobacco to the other cheek and spat. The brown glob sailed between the roan's ears. The old man could sure spit, Brubs noticed; not a drop touched the horse.

Willoughby leaned his bruised torso against Brubs's horse. "Sir," he said, "we'll admit we are new to the wild horse hunting business, but we surely meant you no harm."

"Harm got done." The old man shrugged. "Guess it wouldn't be fair to kill a man for being a greenhorn. Even a stupid one." He lowered the hammer of the Sharps and stowed the weapon in a scabbard slung beneath the stirrup of a heavy, well-worn stock saddle, and glared at Willoughby. "You got a lot to learn about roping, son."

Willoughby winced at a fresh stab of pain through his ribs. "That thought occurred to me, too, sir."

"Mister, you said you'd been workin' that herd for a spell," Brubs said. "You a *mesteñero?*"

"Too dumb to do anything else and too lazy to work." The man on the roan glanced at Willoughby. "You hurt, son?"

Dave flexed his shoulders, flinched at the bite of scrapes and bruises, and shook his head. "I don't think so, sir." He stood, a bit unsteady on shaky legs. "I apologize if we spoiled your hunt. We didn't realize this was your range. If you will be so kind as to excuse us, we'll move on to another area and be out of your way."

"Doubt that," the old-timer said. "You green-horns have got every mustang cavvy around here boogered like you were a pack of lobo wolves." He worked the chew and spat again. "Now that I decided not to kill you — which I may live to regret — I got to figure out what to do with you. Can't leave you charging around the countryside, or every mustanger north of the Rio Grande will starve to death before first frost."

"Well, I been thinkin' about that," Brubs said.

Willoughby moaned. "God help us. He's thinking again."

"Now, mister," Brubs said, "you done figured out we ain't too good at catchin' horses. How's about we team up with you?"

"Team up? With me?" Wiry gray eyebrows went up in surprise. "Why in old billy hell would I want to throw in with a couple of wet-eared whelps who don't know what end of a mustang makes horse apples?"

"We could help," Willoughby said hopefully.

"I've seen your kind of help."

"Mister," Brubs said, his tone gaining enthusiasm as he warmed to the idea, "you learn us how to run mustangs and we help you catch 'em. Why, the three of us workin' as a team could clean Texas plumb out of wild hosses in a couple months. We can easy work out a divvy on the profits."

The old man's brows bunched in thought. He ran the thick fingers of a scarred hand through his wiry beard. He started to shake his head, then hesitated.

"Work out good for you, too," Brubs added eagerly. "You could keep an eye on us. Ain't no better way to make sure we don't mess up no more of your horse hunts."

The old man spat, again. "Maybe you got a point. Somebody's got to teach you younkers something before you spook every mustang from Chihuahua to Canada."

He stepped stiffly from the saddle, strode with a noticeable limp to the two men, and looked both over closely. Then he extended a hand. "Name's Stump Hankins."

"Stump Hankins? I heard of you." Brubs grabbed the hand. "They say up on the Brazos you're the top mustanger in the state, not countin' Comanches. I'm Brubs McCallan." Brubs released his grip and waved toward Dave. "This here's Dave Willoughby."

Willoughby winced as the powerful grip closed on his bruised hand. "It is a pleasure to make your acquaintance, Mr. Hankins."

Stump Hankins cocked an eyebrow at Willoughby. "Son, you sure talk funny."

"He's a Yankee, Mr. Hankins," Brubs broke in, "but he ain't half bad to ride with despite it."

Hankins released his hand, to Willoughby's relief. "I must be getting even dumber in my old age," Hankins groused. "Bucked off on my head in one too many rock piles, I reckon." Then a slight grin creased the bristly beard. "But, what the hell? Watching you two get in wrecks like this one might even pass for entertainment. Call me Stump. My *pa* was *Mr.* Hankins." He spat out a chew of tobacco as big as a man's palm. "If you two greenhorns remember where your camp is, gather your stuff and meet me yonder." He pointed toward a wide, flattop butte standing blue and hazy in the distance.

"Where's yonder?" Willoughby asked.

"Mustang Peak. Country around it's called Mustang Mesa, on account of it's right in the middle of the biggest wild horse herds in Texas. See you there tomorrow."

"Tomorrow? Why not this evening?" Willoughby asked.

Stump Hankins's bushy eyebrows clumped. "How far do you think it is from here to there?"

Willoughby squinted toward the hazy blue butte. "I'd say five, maybe ten miles."

Stump snorted. "It's better than thirty. Near a full day's ride. My camp's on the south end, alongside a creek in a stand of cottonwoods. Can't miss it." The old mustanger limped back to the big roan and swung into the saddle. "You boys might want to sing out before you ride in," he said, "on account of I don't like surprises. Sometimes I get twitchy with that old Sharps." He reined the roan about and set off at a steady trot.

Brubs watched in silence until the old mustanger rounded a bend in the trail and disappeared from view, then turned to Dave. "Stump Hankins," he said, a touch of awe in his voice. "That there man's a legend among us *mesteñeros*. They say up on the Brazos that old man can flat *talk* a horse into comin' right up to him. Heard he catches the real wild ones with nothin' but his teeth — just rides up aside 'em, clamps them jaw teeth on an ear, and gnaws 'em to a stop." Brubs shook his head in wonder. "Partner, I got a feelin' our luck just took a turn for the better here today."

Willoughby started toward the black, limping on a barked shin as he walked. " 'Times go by turns, and chances change by course,' " he muttered aloud, " 'from foul to fair, from better hap to worse.' "

"Say what, partner?"

Willoughby brushed the sand from the black's shoulder, picked up the reins, and cocked an eyebrow at Brubs. "A quote from Robert Southwell, who seemed to be anticipating the turn of my fortunes after I joined up with one Brubs McCallan." He toed the stirrup, swung into the saddle, and moaned aloud. "Let's gather our gear and see if we can find this mustanger's camp."

"Nothin' to worry about," Brubs said nonchalantly, "Stump said we couldn't miss it."

"Where in old billy hell," Stump Hankins grumbled by way of greeting, "have you two greenhorns been?"

"Brubs got lost," Willoughby said.

"Lost?" Brubs's tone was one of wounded indignation. "I never was lost, Dave Willoughby. It's just that they's an awful lot of creeks and cottonwood stands in these parts. Ain't my fault it took a little longer."

Stump Hankins snorted and lowered the Sharps. "Well, maybe it took you two days, but you're here. Where's your packhorse and equipment?"

Willoughby hefted the possibles sack. "This is all we have."

Stump's shaggy head waggled from side to side. "You two are greener than I thought. You came out here to hunt mustangs with nothing but a flour sack full of grub?"

Brubs grinned. "We been travelin' light. Sack's near empty, anyway."

Stump Hankins sighed. "Ride on in. Hitch your horses over there with my string. I'll stir up some grub."

The mustanger's camp had an air of permanence about it, Willoughby thought, as he reined the black around the edge of the clearing. The camp fire was laid on a bed of flat stones, the sandy ground cleared of rocks and fallen limbs. A lean-to built of thin branches around a frame of logs provided shade and shelter from the rains — if it ever rained in this country, he mused. The cottonwoods added a bit of protection from the wind and weather, and a deadfall at the edge of the clearing offered several weeks' supply of firewood within easy reach. A creek rustled through the west side of the camp, its clear waters obviously spring fed, and trickled into a deep pool just beyond the clearing. The site had everything a man needed, Willoughby noted — water, wood, grass for the horses, protection from the elements. A good campsite, and a clean one. Stump apparently had a neat streak in him.

Several large packs and packsaddles lay beside the lean-to. A shovel, a double-bit broadax, and a grubbing hoe leaned against the shelter. Stump's picket line held three horses. Four pack mules were hobbled in a small, grassy meadow beyond the stand of cottonwood trees. The animals were sturdy and had the look of being well-tended. A mule brayed a greeting at Willoughby's black. Stump's big roan gelding backed its ears and nipped at the neck of Brubs's sorrel as the two men stripped the saddles and tied the horses to the line. The scent of frying bacon triggered a rumble in Willoughby's belly before they had finished with the mounts.

Willoughby shouldered the possibles sack, his bedroll and rifle, and followed Brubs back to the camp fire. He saw Brubs cast a quick frown at the digging tools as they strode past the lean-to. The frown faded quickly as Stump forked up bacon and beans, sourdough biscuits from a Dutch oven, and coffee strong enough to float an anvil.

The meal passed mostly in silence, the quiet broken only by an occasional grunt of satisfaction. Finally, after Brubs had put away a second plateful — and with the better part of a biscuit stuck in crumbles to his thick handlebar mustache — the stocky rider leaned back, patted his belly, and grinned.

"You got a way with a skillet, Stump," Brubs said. "If you wasn't so old and ugly, I'd be plumb tempted to ask if you'd marry up with me."

Stump Hankins sniffed in disdain. "Had a damn sight better offers in my time. Now, you two greenhorns start earning your keep. Police up the camp. And mind you, I want my cooking and eating stuff clean, not cowboy camp lick and a promise. Come sunup tomorrow, you get your first class in the Stump Hankins School of Mustang Chousing."

Willoughby felt his pulse quicken at the prospect. "Mr. Hankins, can you give us an idea of what we've been doing wrong?"

Stump pulled a charred pipe from his pocket and reached for his tobacco pouch.

"Everything," he said.

Dave Willoughby eased his black gelding to a stop on a rocky ridge fifteen miles from camp and shifted his weight in the saddle to ease his aching backside. The first week of the Stump Hankins School of Mustang Chousing was turning out to be harder on the butt than a whole year of the hard wooden seats in Dr. Wilfred Von Camp's Examination of Ancient Philosophy class at William and Mary.

And almost as boring.

For five days now they had done nothing but scout the countryside. "Looking for a cavvy you two boneheads haven't already spooked to high heaven," as Stump put it.

Willoughby rubbed his tired rump and blinked against a sudden barrage of sand fired by a gust of hot southwest wind. His eyes felt like he had been on a two-day drunk, or at least what he thought a two-day drunk would feel like. One night was usually enough to cure Dave Willoughby of any extended fascination with the bottle.

The broken countryside that spilled away before him shimmered in the heat. Dust devils spawned by the broiling sun danced through the scrub brush, cactus, and eroded gullies. A buzzard soared overhead, riding the wind on wings that were missing several feathers. The scraggly black bird seemed to be keeping a hopeful eye on Dave.

Willoughby was about to rein the black around when the gelding's ears suddenly perked up. A low, ruffling snort fluttered the black's nostrils. Willoughby squinted in the direction of the black's pointed ears. His heartbeat quickened as he saw the shapes moving through the mesquite and catclaw in the distance, lazing toward the ridge where Dave waited.

He reached down and pressed the black's neck just ahead of the withers, a signal for quiet, and waited patiently as the *manada* of horses inched closer. Willoughby sensed that this was the band they sought, a group of mares led by a blood bay stallion. After a half hour of watching and waiting, he could make out individual animals among the band. He sighed in satisfaction. Stump Hankins had been right; the leggy coyote dun and the brown mule with half an ear missing identified the herd as the one they sought. The *manada* stallion was also as Stump had described him — tall for a mustang, well-muscled, a deep reddish bay. Willoughby wondered for a moment how Hankins could tell which horse was which from the thousands of tracks they had studied around Mustang Mesa, then decided the old man was either very good at his work or some kind of a warlock.

The mustanger's instructions had been brief and to the point. "When you find them, don't run them, and for God's sake, keep the damn rope tied to the saddle. Don't even think about going rope crazy on me. And don't let them see you if you can help it. Just ease on back here, quiet-like. We'll start walking them down in a day or so."

Willoughby waited another ten minutes until he was absolutely sure the *manada* was the one Stump wanted, then reined his black from the ridge and started back toward camp.

Stump Hankins sat cross-legged in front of the lean-to, pulling a rawhide thong through a stirrup leather with his teeth. He glanced up as Dave dismounted.

"I found them, Stump," Willoughby said, aware of the excitement in his voice. "Fifteen miles west of here. The coyote dun, the mule, and the blood bay stallion. About twenty mares in the group."

Hankins grunted in satisfaction. He twisted a knot into the rawhide and tugged at the stirrup leather to make sure the knot would hold, then stood. Willoughby thought he heard the old man's knee joints creak. "Where's your compadre?"

"Swung back to the north a few miles out. Said he was going to scout out the country in that direction."

Hankins nodded and reached for his pipe. "Good. With any luck, he won't find that bunch and spook them. We'll start after them at first light."

"Won't they be miles from there by tomorrow?"

Hankins fired the pipe and squinted through the swirl of smoke at Willoughby. "Nope. Mustangs don't move that much if they don't have to." He shook the match out just before the flame touched his thick fingers. "Territorial animals. Give them enough grass and water, don't booger 'em too much, and they won't range over more than twenty square miles in a season. They'll still be there when we're ready to go get them."

Willoughby led the black away, stripped the saddle, staked the gelding where the horse could easily reach grass and water, and strode back to the camp.

Stump Hankins jabbed his pipe stem toward the camp fire. "Coffee's probably thicker than mud, but it's still hot if you want it." He waited until Willoughby poured himself a cup and squatted beside his bedroll. "You got yourself a passing mark in the first grade of mustanging school, Willoughby," Stump said. "Lesson one is to find the right *manada,* the one with the animals that'll bring the best money. Classes get a little tougher from here on."

Willoughby sipped, winced at the bite of the thick, acidic brew, and watched as the grizzled mustanger started stripping and cleaning his scarred old Sharps rifle. Stump Hankins, it seemed, was always busy — even when it looked like he was just loafing.

"Stump, you said earlier that we'd walk them down. What did you mean by that?"

Hankins worried the pipe for a moment, raising a cloud of blue-white smoke that looked like a tiny cannon had just gone off. "Tell you about it when your partner gets back," the voice from the cloud said. "Never did care much for spinning the same yarn twice."

Willoughby sat in silence as he finished his coffee, then stood, stretched, and scraped a palm across the wiry stubble of his cheek. "I'm a couple of days west of a bath and shave. Think I'll go down to the pool and wash off a few layers."

Hankins glanced up and shook his head. "No

bath." He drew on the pipe, spat, and rapped the bowl against a knee to knock the spittle from the stem. "Mustang's got a better sense of smell than a mountain lion. They can pick up a man's scent a half mile off when the wind's right. Until we get them caught, you don't even change your underdrawers." He put the pipe down and ran a patch through the bore of the rifle. "We want them to get used to our smell before we try to pen them. Otherwise, they'll spook to high heaven all over again."

Willoughby winced inwardly, aware of the dirt, sweat, and horse scent of his own body. He was ripe. Dave Willoughby had been brought up to believe in a bath at least three times a week. His army days under a spit-and-polish commander had reinforced his aversion to grime.

At least, he mused, Stump's bathwater ban wasn't likely to upset Brubs much. The only time Brubs voluntarily got near soap was when a woman was in his plans. And only then if she was picky about it, Brubs had pointed out.

Brubs rode in just before sundown, his face streaked with dust and sweat, a big grin under the bushy mustache.

"See anything out there, McCallan?" Stump asked by way of greeting.

"Six rattlers, four tarantulas, and forty miles of empty. Thought once I saw three cantinas and five pretty Mexican señoritas," Brubs said, "but that turned out to be one of them mirages. Just had me a nice, relaxin' horseback ride. Cut lots of sign but didn't see no mustangs."

Stump grunted. "Where there's tracks, there's mustangs. That country'll keep. Willoughby found the bunch we're after. We'll start working on them tomorrow."

Excitement flared in Brubs's eyes. "Good stock?"

"Best *manada* in the whole of Mustang Mesa. They'll bring a good price."

Brubs rubbed his palms together. "Boy, I can already feel them gold coins." He winked at Willoughby. "See, partner? I told you to stick with old Brubs and you'd get rich."

Stump fed a couple of fresh mesquite limbs into the camp fire. "Don't go spending it all just yet," he said. "We've got to catch them first. Gather around, children. Lesson two in the Stump Hankins School of Mustang Chousing is about to begin."

Dave Willoughby rode slumped in the saddle, exhaustion heavy on his shoulders. His head throbbed from constant squinting in the near pitch-darkness of the night; only starlight penetrated the moonless sky. His knees ached. He had lost the feeling in his backside three hours ago, and his left forearm was trying to cramp from his steady grip on the reins. He had been ten hours in the saddle and covered better than forty miles, as best he could calculate.

Mustang Mesa, he thought, looked like what the back side of the moon must be. The starlight turned rockfalls and mesquite clumps into ominous black lumps, malevolent creatures waiting to pounce on any horseman fool enough to ride the night through. Shale and sand washes were as treacherous as deep canyons in the blackness. Badger holes lurked unseen to trap a hoof, while catclaw, cactus, and mesquite thorns leapt from the darkness to grab at arms and legs. Willoughby tried to shake off the eerie sensation triggered by the black-on-black landscape, trusting his horse to find the safest trail and best footing.

The Stump Hankins School of Mustang Chousing was a lot less glamorous than Willoughby had expected.

The three men had been walking the blood bay's band for four days and four nights, making no move to run after the wild horses. The trick, Stump said, was to keep up a steady, relentless pressure on the mustangs.

"Horses are like men," Stump had said. "They've got to have sleep. Mustangs nap three times during the night, at about nine o'clock, at eleven, and then a couple of hours just before daylight. One of these mustangs can go a far piece without water and farther than that without grass, but they have to have their sleep. Keep them awake and on the move, and we'll have dog-tired and sore-footed horses. And that, children, is the only way to catch mustangs."

Stump hadn't bothered to mention that the men would be as dog-tired as the wild horses.

Stump had taken the saddle for the first day and night, partly because he did not completely trust his helpers' abilities to track in the dark, and partly to get the lay of the mustang band's range. Willoughby and Brubs took turns the next two days and nights, riding in twelve-hour shifts, keeping the mustangs on the move but still letting them stop long enough to drink. Stump had been emphatic about that. Mustangs with their bellies full of water had to work harder and couldn't run as fast as a band that been "dried out," he said. Willoughby had worried about being able to find Brubs and the wild band when his turn as walker came, but the old warlock of a mustanger surprised him again. Stump had told him where the horses would be at a given time — and he pegged it to within a half mile.

For the first couple of days the routine had been the same. The blood bay stallion would spot the horseman, take a few steps forward, paw the ground, shake its head, then wheel and nip the mares into a run. The walker on horseback pursued, but at a leisurely pace to save his own mount's stamina. When the *manada* fled from sight, the hunter followed their tracks until the band was once again in view.

Now the pressure was obviously taking its toll. The *manada* seldom ran. Sore feet and exhaustion had more to do with that than growing familiarity with the men on horseback, Willoughby realized. But now the band allowed the pursuers to get a bit closer every day before fleeing, and

110

even then they moved only in a listless trot. Willoughby felt sympathy for the wild horses. He knew how it felt to be badgered and beleaguered. He had had enough of that back home.

He kneed his horse into a slow trot as the distant black shapes slowed. It was the third time tonight they had tried to stop. Willoughby didn't need to study the stars to tell what time it was. The horses were as accurate as any clock. The third stop meant it was two hours before dawn.

Willoughby had moved to within a hundred yards of the band before the one-eared mule brayed an alarm. The blood bay stallion nipped at the haunches of two hipshot mares, urging them into a shambling trot. Willoughby checked his mount back to an easy walk. His job was done, for the moment. The *manada* was on the move again; there would be no rest for the mustangs tonight. Whenever they looked back or tried to stop, he would be there.

At first, Willoughby had been astonished that the mustang stallion would permit the presence of the mule and the coyote dun in his band. Now he understood what Stump had said. Wild horses had an affinity for mules because the long-eared creatures were one of nature's best watchdogs, often spotting trouble before any of the mustangs did. And mules had an instinct for finding water in dry times.

As for the coyote dun, Stump had been close enough to the horse once to see that it was a gelding. The stallion would fight another stud to the death to keep his harem of mares together, but the blood bay knew there was no threat from the neutered male horse. The coyote dun also wore an interesting mix of Mexican and American brands, Stump said. That meant the gelding was likely a strayed ranch horse, broken to saddle and trained. And that made him even more valuable to a buyer. The brands wouldn't matter, Stump said. It didn't take long to put a fresh brand on an animal.

Willoughby shifted his weight in the saddle and struggled to keep himself alert despite the aching weariness in his bones. The Mustang Mesa country held more than just wild horses. Cougars, the big cats that Stump called "painters," often prowled the region, preying on mustang foals. Willoughby had heard the cry of a panther a couple of nights ago. It was a blood-chilling scream that raised the hairs on a man's forearms, a screech that sounded like a woman in agony. Willoughby decided on the spot he wanted no part of any cougar. Brubs wanted to rope one. But then, Brubs did have a sort of a wild hair, Dave mused. What Brubs planned to do with the cat once he had it roped, Willoughby didn't know, but he would have given his last dollar to watch the wreck that was sure to follow.

Even worse than the cats, Stump said, were the occasional bands of bandits, Mexican and Anglo alike, who drifted into and out of the area. And still worse, he added, were the renegade bands of Indians — Chiricahua Apaches and wide-ranging Comanches — who bolted the reservations and sought refuge from army troops in the wild, rugged land. One of the night walker's jobs was to keep a sharp eye out for any signs of human life. A distant speck of light could be the camp fire of a bandit gang or a raiding party of bronco Indians. Maybe, Willoughby told himself, that was one reason the night seemed ominous.

He shrugged the thoughts aside. A man could get killed back East, too. He concentrated on following the mustangs. A couple more days, Stump said, and they would have their first catch of wild horses penned.

Willoughby smiled. That, he thought, might be something like Brubs's roping a cougar. Once you'd caught them, how did you turn them loose? He had an idea that might take a couple more lessons from the Hankins School of Mustanging.

Stump Hankins shook Brubs McCallan awake, none too gently. "Off your back and on your feet, younker," Stump grumbled. "No sense sleeping away the whole day."

Brubs glanced at the sky. It was still pitch-black, a good two hours before sunup. Every muscle in his body seemed stiff and sore. "Never could figure out," Brubs grumbled, "why you cranky old wore-out codgers can't stand seein' a tired man get his beauty rest. Dust must have got into what brains them mustangs left you."

"Quit your bellyaching and roll out of those soogans, McCallan," Stump growled back. "Nobody but a top-shelf whore ever got rich lying down. We got work to do."

Brubs crawled from the blankets and scrubbed chapped knuckles across bleary eyes. "What we been doin' ain't work?"

"Depends on how you look at it," Stump said. "Where in the world would you rather be than out here on the open range, enjoying the feel of a good horse between your knees, smelling the clean, fresh air of the great outdoors, and passing the hours in the fine companionship of two bosom buddies?"

Brubs grunted again. "I'd about as soon be in a Nuevo Laredo parlor house right now, with a nice-lookin' young Mexican señorita fetchin' my coffee." Brubs raised an eyebrow at Stump. "When you get so damn cheerful so early in the mornin', Stump, I get downright twitchy. You figurin' on pullin' some kind of dirty trick today, ain't you?"

Stump fed fresh sticks to the fire and reached for a skillet. "Today starts a whole new lesson in mustanging school, friend McCallan," he said as he sliced thick slabs of bacon into the skillet. "Today we get ready to catch us some wild horses."

Brubs pulled on his boots and came to his feet, brought fully awake by the aroma of fresh coffee and a quick surge of anticipation. "We gonna rope a bunch of 'em today?"

Stump shook his head. "Nope. Better. We set up so we can catch the whole *manada* in a day or two. Better load up good on breakfast this morning. You may need it."

Brubs ate quickly, his hunger fueled by growing excitement. Stump Hankins reached for Brubs's plate when he had finished. "I'll take care of the camp chores this morning," he said. "You put the packs on a couple of mules." He waved toward the tools beside the lean-to. "Be sure and pack that shovel, grubbing hoe, and ax."

Brubs stiffened in alarm. "Shovel? Grubbin' hoe? What we need them for?"

Stump grinned. "Today you turn a new page in the dramatic and exciting life of a *mesteñero*, McCallan. You and me are going to build a catch pen while Dave puts a few more miles on those horses."

"Catch pen?" Brubs felt a chill down his spine. "Build it? With them things?"

"Can't pen mustangs without a pen. It won't be so bad. Not more than twelve, fourteen hours of digging and chopping, we'll have it ready. I got the place for it picked out."

Brubs shuddered visibly. He could almost feel the blisters rising on his palms. "You old coot," he said, "I knew you was plannin' some outrage."

SIX

Brubs McCallan leaned against the handle of the double-bit ax and studied the broken blister on his left palm. Sweat trickled down his wrists and stung the raw flesh as if he had stuck his hand into a bed of red ants. His shoulders ached, his arms felt like lead weights, and his feet hurt.

"Might as well of stayed in San 'Tone," he grumbled. "Least there they'd let the prisoners stop choppin' cotton long enough to eat."

"Quit dawdling, McCallan," Stump Hankins said as he lashed a mesquite limb between two shoulder-high junipers. "We still got lots of daylight left."

Brubs cast a cranky glance at the mustanger. "You got a mean streak in you wider'n the Brazos, Stump Hankins," he groused. "Work a man plumb down like a wind-broke horse. I come out here to keep my hands *off* a hickory handle." He flexed his stiff fingers. "These hands was meant to stroke female flesh, not no ax handle."

Stump tugged the lashings tight and spat a stream of tobacco juice. The glob splattered onto a horned toad's back. The little lizard jumped, shook its head in indignant outrage, then scurried out of sight. "You were the one

116

wanted to be a mustanger. This is part of the fun."

"Seems an awful damn lot like work to me."

Stump reached for another mesquite limb. "Never promised you a bed of petunias to lie in. You want to make enough money for some of that female skin, you got to work at least a little bit now and then."

Brubs wondered how much work Stump Hankins would consider a lot. But the old man with the bum knee and knocked down shoulder had done more than his share of the chopping and hauling and still looked like he could do another day's worth without stopping. In fact, he had just about worked Brubs into the ground and had barely broken a sweat in the process. Stump Hankins was a tough old bird.

Stump pointed the mesquite limb toward Brubs. "Axes weren't built to lean on. The sooner we get this thing done, the sooner we can quit."

Brubs sighed and picked up the ax. It seemed to weigh about forty pounds. He stood for a moment, surveying the day's work. The catch pen itself was finished. The only trail out the far end of the narrow canyon was fenced off with heavy logs snaked from a stand of cottonwoods along a draw a quarter mile away. Other logs lay alongside the mouth of the canyon, waiting to be shoved into place as a makeshift gate to trap the horses inside. The canyon walls formed the rest of the catch pen, steep cliffs more than fifty feet high. A horse would have to be at least half mountain goat to climb up those walls.

Now, as the sun slipped midway down the western sky, the two men were nearing completion of the wings — small cottonwood and mesquite posts supporting a loose web of brush and limbs. The wings ran in a V shape from the mouth of the canyon outward more than a hundred yards. The makeshift barriers would steer the mustang *manada* into the canyon and captivity. It looked like a shaky proposition to Brubs. Any half-starved jackass could jump the brush or just plow through the wings and keep going. But Stump said it wasn't in a mustang's nature to buck a barrier when the way in front was clear.

"Mustangs are dumber than the men who chase them," Stump had said, "and the good Lord knows that doesn't make them just real long on brains."

Brubs swung the ax blade against the trunk of a gnarled mesquite the size of a man's leg. The impact of bit against the tough green wood sent a jolt through his arms and shoulders. Sweat trickled from his forehead into his eyes and set them to smarting, blurring his vision. The ache in his back grew worse with each swing of the ax. After what seemed an eternity, the mesquite trunk gave way with a creak. The twisted tree slowly toppled.

Brubs paused for a breath and flexed his back.

He was getting a painful knot between his shoulder blades.

Stump Hankins reached for the ax. "I'll whittle down a couple more. That'll give us plenty. You work on setting up the rest of this wing fence. It doesn't have to be tight. Just think like a mustang and quit when you reckon it looks solid enough."

There was an hour's daylight left when Stump Hankins finally stepped back, surveyed the work with a critical eye, and pronounced the catch pen and wings done. "She'll hold, I reckon."

Brubs sank onto an empty packsaddle, his muscles trembling in exhaustion. " 'Bout time you had some good news. I ain't been this wore out since that little redhead up in Denton finally decided to turn me loose."

"Don't get just real comfortable too quick," Stump said. He glanced at the sun. "It'll be time for you to relieve Willoughby as walker soon."

Brubs groaned aloud. "That mean streak of yours just couldn't stay hid, could it?"

Stump squatted beside the flimsy brush wing and stuffed his pipe. "I want you riding drag on that *manada* when we pen them tomorrow. Old Dave's a likable feller and learning fast, but I don't think he's got as much horse savvy as you — even if you haven't showed it yet." He scratched a sulphur match on a boot sole and fired the pipe. "I'll take the east point and turn them toward the wings. Dave'll have the west flank."

Brubs felt a quiver of anticipation despite the heavy fatigue in his muscles. "We pen them horses tomorrow?"

Stump said, "Lord willing and the herd doesn't spill. You best ride that big roan of mine tomorrow. Old Choctaw has forgot more about mustanging than you'll ever know. If you don't get in his way too much, *he'll* pen them."

Brubs McCallan caught his second wind at first light.

He wasn't sure if it was the sight of the mustang band at close range, or the sudden quiver of alertness in the tall, deep-cheated roan between his knees that brought him fully awake and chased the weariness from his bones.

Stump Hankins had been right, as usual, about the horse called Choctaw. Throughout the night the big roan had shambled along, ears flopped like a mule's and about half asleep, but always the same distance behind the *manada*. Now the gelding's ears perked forward, he tongued the bit, and Brubs could feel the nervous excitement in Choctaw's solid muscles. The wings of the catch pen were less than a half mile ahead, and the roan seemed to know that this was the day it was to be put to use.

The mustangs were closer now than ever, not more than forty yards ahead of Brubs. For the first time since the walk-down began days ago, Brubs could make out the individual markings of the animals clearly with the coming of dawn.

120

The wild horses moved slowly, favoring tender hooves, heads carried low. The lead mare, a deep-chested brown with her belly beginning to swell from the foal she carried, was still out front. The one-eared mule was at her left hip, as always. The blood bay stallion trailed the *manada*, halfheartedly nipping at the rumps of stragglers but stumbling in exhaustion himself.

Brubs's belly twitched as the blood bay wheeled, shook his head, pawed the ground, and took a couple of halting steps toward the roan. Brubs fought back the urge to turn Choctaw. Stump had told him the stud was likely to try to run a bluff when pursuit got too close and he was near the end of his endurance. Of course, Stump casually added, sometimes they weren't bluffing.

Choctaw didn't seem worried, so Brubs left the big roan alone. The stud snorted a couple of times, then turned and trotted back to the *manada*. Brubs breathed a silent sigh of relief. Getting caught in the middle of a horse fight wasn't his idea of a good time Saturday night.

He trailed the band another four hundred yards before the one-eared mule suddenly looked up toward the east, then brayed. Brubs glanced in that direction and felt his heartbeat pick up. Stump Hankins had topped the ridge, silhouetted against the early morning sun.

The lead mare stopped, stared toward the horseman on the ridge for a few seconds, snorted, and turned north. Brubs fought back the urge to yelp in triumph; the mustangs were headed straight toward the wings of the trap, and they were flanked. Willoughby had moved into position at Brubs's left, ready to turn the herd if the mustangs tried to bolt to the west. Stump had warned the two in no uncertain terms that now was the time to take it easy. "Don't go chousing them unless you have to," Stump had said.

Brubs felt the excitement and tension mount as the mustangs neared the trap. The lead mare was almost inside the brush fences now, moving cautiously. A younger horse, a black yearling with a white snip on its nose, peeled from the herd and started trotting away. Choctaw lifted into a slow lope, headed the yearling, and turned it back into the herd, all without a cue from his rider. Brubs made a mental note to try to trade Stump out of the savvy roan. He didn't think he could pull it off. Stump Hankins knew a good mustanging horse was worth more than a half dozen riders in this trade.

The blood bay moved at a sore-footed trot back and forth behind his band, nervous and suspicious, but made no move to bolt. Brubs took up his rope, tied fast to the horn, and shook out a loop, just in case. He halfway hoped one of the mustangs would make a break. Roping was a lot more fun than chopping mesquites.

The mustangs disappointed him.

They seemed too tired to notice that the brush fences had narrowed as they trudged toward the mouth of the canyon. Only the mule seemed to be getting a bit twitchy, but he showed no inclination to leave the brown lead mare's side. Willoughby rode a few yards to Brubs's left now. Stump had the right flank just inside the wing.

Ten minutes later, Stump and Willoughby slid the last gate pole into place.

"Well, children," Stump said casually as he leaned against the top pole, "here's your first catch. A few dozen more and you'll earn your spurs as *mesteñeros*."

Brubs swung down from Choctaw and studied the horses in the catch pen. The blood bay stud squealed, pawed the ground, and turned to glare at the three men, the whites of his eyes showing. Up close, Brubs could see the numerous battle scars that laced the stallion's hide. The bay snorted and backed his ears, took a few mincing steps toward the men, then stopped, tossed his head and squealed before whirling back to the band.

The other mustangs milled for a few moments, then stood hipshot, heads down, too tired to graze or drink.

All the hard work and the aching muscles seemed worth it now, Brubs thought. His heart pounded like it was Saturday night and payday.

"What do you think they're worth, Stump?" Willoughby asked.

Stump squinted at the *manada* for a few minutes, then grunted. "Average probably fifteen a head. The good mares will bring twenty, twenty-five apiece." He fished in his pocket for a plug of tobacco, gnawed off a chew, and tucked it into a cheek. "These mares as a group are better than most you'll find," he said. "Most mustang studs are like you flat-bellied young sprouts who'll jump on anything that's female. This one seems to be either a sight more picky about his women, or just plain lucky."

Brubs turned his attention from the stallion for a closer look at the coyote dun. The gelding was the color of fresh-skimmed cream with a black mane and tail. A dark stripe ran along the back, and all four legs were black from the knees down. But look past the color and the dun had to be the ugliest horse Brubs had ever seen, even if he ignored the three American and two Spanish brands on the horse's hips and shoulders.

Brubs cocked an eyebrow at Stump. "Thought you said that coyote dun was the best of the bunch," he said. "He's pigeon-toed, cow-hocked, he's got a rump sharper'n a roadrunner's tail, he's dish-faced, Roman-nosed, one eye's cloudy, and he's got a head so long it looks like he'd have to rear up to eat. Don't look like much of a horse to me."

Stump worried the tobacco for a moment, then spat. "McCallan, you can't judge a horse from its looks no more than you can judge a woman. Best whore I ever bedded was ugly enough to stop a Union Pacific locomotive dead on the tracks on a downhill grade." He nodded toward the dun, which dozed, ears aflop, at one side of the *manada.* "That animal's one of the type the Mexicans call *puros Españoles,* pure Spanish. Never saw a coyote dun that didn't have a lot of bottom and an excess of smart."

"I didn't think color meant much where horses were concerned," Willoughby said.

"Some say it doesn't. I think it does. Never trust a pure white horse, unless you're a young Comanche buck looking for big medicine. Got to keep an eye on blood bays, too, like that stud. Mean streak in them." Stump scraped a gob of horse manure from a boot against the lower gate rail. "Every cowman who's forked one of those coyote duns will tell you the same thing. They're natural cow ponies, and they'll go all day on a cup of water and half a biscuit. Bring top dollar from any man who puts cow sense over pretty. More than that from a Mexican. A vaquero will trade his prettiest daughter for a coyote dun. A bandit looking for something that'll cover lots of ground quick will slit your gizzard for one."

Brubs sniffed in disbelief. "He sure don't look like much."

"He probably thinks the same about you, McCallan," Stump said. "With those brands and that saddle-scald scar just behind the withers, that horse is broke to ride. That'll save you two younkers some work."

"Speaking of which," Willoughby said, "now that we've caught them, what do we do with them?"

Stump lifted an eyebrow at Dave. "Children,

that's a whole 'nuther chapter in the Hankins School of Mustang Chousing. Might as well start your studies right now." He slipped the old Sharps from the saddle scabbard and cocked the hammer.

"What's with the buffalo gun?" Brubs asked.

"That stud's *caballo de muerte* — a death horse, killer for sure." He lifted the rifle.

Brubs clapped a hand over the rear sight of the weapon. "Wait a minute! You fixin' to shoot that stud?"

"Just as quick as you move your damn paw off my rifle," Stump growled.

"Stump, you can't do that! That there's a valuable horse — you seen the kind of colts he throws. He's gotta be worth sixty, maybe a hundred dollars!"

Stump glowered at Brubs. "I guess you've got a better idea?"

"You bet your butt I have," Brubs said. "You give me that stud, Stump. I'll have him eatin' out of my hand in a day's time."

Stump lowered the rifle. A wry grin replaced the frown on his grizzled face. "You must be a hell of a hand with the rough string, McCallan."

"I can handle anything with horsehair on it."

Stump waved a hand toward the bay. "Then, by all means, be my guest. Watching you get stomped to death might be good entertainment."

Brubs started to toe the stirrup.

"Not on my horse, McCallan," Stump said. "I wouldn't whimper real loud watching you get killed, but I'd sure hate to see Choctaw get hurt. You want that stud, you get him afoot or let me shoot him and save you some grief."

Brubs cast a withering glance at the old mustanger, then handed the reins to Willoughby and shook out a loop in his rope.

"Brubs," Willoughby said cautiously, "I think we'd best pay attention to Stump. He hasn't misled us yet."

"I ain't throwin' away that much money just 'cause some old coot's boogered by a horse." He sniffed in disdain. "Death horse. Silliest thing I ever heard." He climbed through the gate poles.

"Brubs, watch out," Willoughby warned. His eyes were narrowed, his brow wrinkled in worry.

"Partner, I know what I'm doin'," Brubs said. "You just watch and old Brubs McCallan'll show you how to handle a *real* hoss."

Brubs paused for a moment, rope in hand. The blood bay stood a few feet from a canyon wall, the base littered by fallen boulders. The canyon floor was reasonably level and clear of obstructions. All he had to do now was get close enough to the bay stud to put a loop around his neck.

The stallion pawed the ground, ears pointed toward Brubs. Brubs started talking as he eased a couple of steps closer to the bay. "Easy now, boy," he said. "I don't plan to hurt you none. Just stand there like a gentle milk cow so's you and me can get acquainted."

The bay's ears flicked back and forth as he watched the man on the ground move closer. "Atta boy," Brubs said softly, "I knowed you was gentle enough. Come to Brubs now. Come to Papa."

The stallion shook its head, tossing the long forelock away from its eyes. "Don't go gettin' boogery on me now, Red," Brubs said soothingly. "Just stand right where you're at, like the good horse you're going to be. I reckon you'll make somebody a passel of mighty good colts." The bay's ears flattened back against the thick, heavily muscled neck. "Steady, now," Brubs said. "Just think about all them prime fillies you're goin' to get without no work at all. They'll just lead 'em out to you. All the females you'd ever want."

Brubs's confidence grew as he eased to within a few feet of the stallion, the hemp rope resting easy and comfortable in his hand.

The bay suddenly wheeled away. Brubs whirled the rope overhead once and made his throw. The loop settled over the stallion's head. Brubs yanked the slack, wrapped the loose end of the lariat around his hips, and braced himself for the shock when the horse hit the end of the rope.

The jolt never came.

The bay came to a sliding stop at the touch of the rope, then turned to face Brubs, the whites of his eyes prominent in the deep red. Brubs grinned. "Well, I'll be damned, Red," he said, "I reckon you been roped before —"

The bay bared his teeth and charged.

Brubs barked a curse, dodged the horse's teeth by a half inch, and felt the thump of a solid shoulder into his side. The impact staggered him, almost knocked him down. He caught his balance and ducked aside as a front hoof whistled past his ear and sent his hat flying. The stallion wheeled and launched a powerful kick with a hind foot. The hoof barely missed Brubs's ribs. Brubs stumbled backward, trying to get clear of the snapping teeth and cracking hooves. He caught a glancing kick on a shoulder, a numbing blow that felt like it had taken his arm off. The impact sent him sprawling six feet from two big boulders at the base of the canyon wall. Brubs rolled, scrambled to his feet, and sprinted toward the opening between the rocks. He yelped as the stallion's teeth took away half a hip pocket and a layer of hide, and dove the last yard into the space between the boulders. He wedged his body as far back into the rocks as it would go; a pawing front hoof scraped against a boulder by Brubs's side and the massive jaws snapped only inches from his neck. Brubs thrust out an arm, instinctively trying to ward off the furious attack.

"For Christ's sake," Brubs yelled as he dodged another snap from the yellowed teeth, "somebody shoot this crazy son of a bitch!"

The blood bay's teeth scraped across Brubs's forearm. Brubs steeled himself for the blow of a hoof as the stallion reared high above.

The stud's body suddenly went sideways at the meaty slap of a heavy caliber slug; a puff of dust flew from the blood bay's shoulder as the muzzle blast of Stump's Sharps Fifty boomed down the canyon. The horse went down, kicking, then struggled to its feet and turned toward Brubs, teeth bared. Another slap sounded a split second before the sharp crack of Willoughby's Winchester. The bay's knees collapsed; the horse fell straight down, legs beneath it, the head with its still-bared teeth landing with a painfully solid thump on Brubs's leg.

Brubs lay for a moment, gasping for breath, his heart pounding against his chest. He vaguely heard the rumble of hooves and squeals as the rest of the mustang band, spooked by the gunshots, thundered toward the far end of the small canyon. He could only lie back against the rough boulder and stare in disbelief at the blood bay's head atop his leg. The sheer terror of the last few seconds slowly passed, giving way to the first stings of pain from the bruises and scrapes. He lifted his gaze at the sound of footsteps approaching on the run. Willoughby skidded to a stop beside the dead stallion. "You all right, Brubs? Are you hurt?"

"Damn fool question." Brubs's voice was shaky. "I just been bit, kicked, run over, and stomped by a damn horse. On top of that I think I peed in my pants."

"He's all right, Stump," Willoughby called

130

over his shoulder. "He's bitching. That's a good sign." He turned back to Brubs. "Anything broken?"

"Don't think so. You want to drag that idiot stud's head off my leg, we'll find out."

Stump casually sauntered up a moment later and stood looking down at Brubs, palms crossed over the muzzle of the Sharps. "One thing's sure," the old mustanger said. "He didn't get his brains kicked out. Weren't any to start with."

Brubs snapped a cold glance at the old mustanger. "You old coot, why didn't you shoot that crazy son of a bitch quicker?"

"You didn't ask quicker."

"I was pretty damn busy there for a while." Brubs flexed his left hand. It still worked, but it hurt like blazes. Blood soaked what was left of his shirtsleeve, and the raw spot where the bay had bit the skin from his butt stung something fierce. He sighed in relief as Willoughby lifted the dead horse's head far enough to let Brubs slip his bruised leg free. He stared at the dead stallion for a moment. "That damn fool horse tried to kill me."

"Saw right off what was going to happen," Stump said.

"You sure didn't bust your britches tryin' to stop it," Brubs grumped.

"Man's determined to play with rattlers, that's his business," Stump said. His gray eyes held an amused twinkle. "Figured if you weren't too keen on listening to your human teacher I'd just let the stud run the class."

Willoughby slipped a hand under Brubs's shoulders and helped him to his feet. Both legs hurt, but he was able to stand.

"Had a stud come after me like that once," Stump said casually. "That's where I got this bum shoulder. Still got tooth marks on my leg, too. Took five slugs from a handgun to get him off me. Can you walk?"

Brubs grunted. "Reckon so, but I sure ain't up to no footrace. Them other horses bust out from the shootin'?"

"No. They just made a couple circles around the canyon and quit. Too tired to try and break through a fence." Stump ran a practiced gaze over Brubs. "Looks like you lost a little skin, but nothing serious. You'll mend. When we get back to camp, we'll smear a little bacon grease on the raw spots." Stump shouldered the rifle. "Come along, children. We still got work to do."

"Dammit, Stump," Brubs growled, "I told you not to use them dirty words like work in front of me."

Brubs McCallan came awake slowly, as tired as if he'd worked all night.

The night sky told him it was still a couple of hours before dawn, but Dave was already up and stirring. Brubs heard the clink of the coffeepot lid and Dave Willoughby's soft humming, but he wasn't ready yet to try to roll out of his blankets and face another day.

132

The raw spots on Brubs's body still stung, especially the horse bite on his butt. Sweat and saddle leather chafe wasn't giving his rump a chance to heal. His muscles were stiff and sore yet from the encounter with the blood bay almost a week ago. Stump Hankins hadn't cut him much slack for healing time. They had started working the mustangs the morning after the stud tried to peel Brubs — hot, dirty work that had cost Brubs another layer of skin here and there.

At least he had gotten to do a little roping, which helped take his mind off his miseries for a time. Stump showed them how to clog the more skittish mares, cutting forked sticks and binding the fork just above the mares' fetlocks. The clog left them free to walk, but if they tried to break into a run their back feet would come down on the trailing end of the forked stick and trip them. "A few days under clog and they'll be as gentle and easy to handle as a backyard goat," Stump said.

Willoughby had questioned the need for clogs. "It seems there should be a more humane way," he said. "Those sticks will make the horses' ankles pretty sore."

"We could make it easy on ourselves and knee them, like some mustangers do," Stump said. "Stick a knife in their knee joints and drain off the fluid, they sure couldn't run. But I never did hold with crippling a perfectly good horse on purpose. Seems downright inhuman to treat an animal that way."

Brubs grumbled to himself that Stump Hankins showed a lot more consideration for the horses than he showed his partners, but he stopped short of saying so. He had to admit he was learning the mustang business in a hurry under the old man's guidance.

Along with the clogging, they had branded the animals. Stump used an inverted horseshoe as his brand. Brubs would have preferred something with a little more style, maybe a brand that would hint at the three-man partnership. But he didn't argue. After he and Willoughby built their stake and set out on their own they could come up with a classier iron.

The mares had quickly stopped fighting the clogs and settled down to water and graze in the canyon.

The coyote dun didn't need clogging. He had spent a couple of days in hobbles, then switched to the picket line. The ugly dun had promptly taken up with Willoughby's black. The two were like lifelong buddies now, watering and grazing together. The dun nickered and paced back and forth on the picket every time Willoughby rode the black out of the dun's sight.

Brubs shifted and moaned, drawing a glance from Dave, who had his face lathered and a straight razor in hand. Brubs never had understood Willoughby's passion for water and chopping off perfectly good whiskers, especially out here in the middle of nowhere without a señorita in fifty miles. But, Brubs supposed, every man had his own strange little quirks.

Brubs lifted a hand and studied his freshly scraped knuckles. "Mornin', partner," he said. "Hope the sound of me tryin' to grow skin didn't bother your sleep none." He glanced around camp. "Stump ain't back yet?"

Willoughby scraped the razor down his cheek. It sounded to Brubs like the razor needed a good stropping. Or Dave needed softer whiskers.

"Not yet," Willoughby said. "He said it might take him two days to get supplies from Laredo and another couple of days to scout the countryside for more mustangs, now that we've got these reasonably tame. He's been gone four days, so he should be back any time."

"What we need more mustangs for? We got better'n twenty head already, countin' the mule and that catfish-ugly dun. Seems like that ought to be enough."

Willoughby swished the razor in a pan of water, ran his free hand over his chin, and swiped at a patch of whiskers that had dodged the blade on the first pass. "Stump said this is probably going to be his last trip out as a *mesteñero,* and he wanted to make it a profitable one. He says as long as he's got some help, he might as well make use of it."

Brubs yawned, started to stretch, and winced at the fresh aches awakened by the movement. "At least the old coot's started calling us help instead of greenhorns."

"As a matter of fact, he told me just before

he rode out that you were turning into a fair hand," Willoughby said. "He also told me he'd break my neck if I told you what he said."

For some reason Brubs couldn't understand, the comment made him feel better. He'd gotten attached to the crusty old mossback. The camp felt sort of empty without him. "Stump still got that itch in his britches about gatherin' in a bunch of young studs?"

"Yes. He says if we can get a dozen or more good young mustangs, geld them, and break them to saddle, we'll make quite a sum of money for a few weeks' work." He finished shaving, rinsed and stowed the razor, and tossed the soapy water aside.

"Dave, what you gonna do with your share of the mustang money?"

Willoughby frowned. "To tell you the truth, I never gave it much thought beyond some new clothes and a haircut. You?"

A quick grin lifted Brubs's lips. "Buy me a soft bed for a day or so. Then all the whiskey and women I can handle."

"*Carpe diem,*" Willoughby said wryly as he lifted the coffeepot lid and dropped in a lump of leftover grounds.

"There you go with that foreign lingo again," Brubs said. "Talk American. What's it mean?"

"It translates roughly as 'seize the day.' It's a Latin phrase. You might say it's Brubs McCallan's motto." He cocked an eyebrow at his partner. "Seriously, Brubs, don't you think we ought to consider investing the money? I was thinking of railroad stocks, and perhaps a few shares in a powder manufacturing plant. Those two industries have a good record of paying steady and substantial dividends."

Brubs shook his head incredulously. "You mean just hand it over to some round-bellied jasper who never did a day's work in his life? I wouldn't trust any man wearin' a silk suit and store-bought shoes with my money. Them folks'll rob you quicker'n a bandit and expect you to thank 'em for the pleasure of gettin' your wallet raped." He struggled stiffly into his boots, then cast a wary glance at Willoughby. "You ain't fixin' to turn town boy on me, are you?"

Willoughby listened to the first few glugs from the coffeepot, then shrugged. "I don't know. I thought maybe someday I'd settle down, find a nice girl, get married, and maybe have some kids."

"Dave Willoughby," Brubs squawked in indignation, "I told you not to use no bad language like that around me. Marry? To *one* woman? And kids?" He shook his head in mock despair. "You been gettin' too much sun, amigo. I got to start watchin' you closer. You may be goin' loco on me. Coffee ready?"

"Just about. Let's give it another five minutes or so. This is the third day we've used these same grounds. They're starting to lose a bit of flavor." Willoughby reached for a skillet.

"What's your breakfast order? You have two choices this morning — stale bacon and leftover biscuits, or leftover biscuits and stale bacon."

Brubs snorted. "Gimme the stale bacon and leftover biscuits."

"An excellent choice, sir. Specialty of the house."

"Wish I'd of cut a hindquarter off that damn blood bay stud and made jerky out of it," Brubs grumped. "Then ever' time I went into the mesquites to squat, I'd grin at what was left of that fool horse."

A half smile touched Willoughby's lips. "The jerky would probably have been too tough to chew." He sliced the greenish-gray spots from a couple of thick slabs of bacon and dropped the cuts in the skillet.

"Yeah. Probably give me the green-apple trots, too. Hustle up with that bacon, amigo. My gut just rumbled."

Stump Hankins rode in an hour before sundown astride the leggy roan called Choctaw, leading a mule laden with packs. He waved toward the mule.

"Fresh grub, boys. Even managed to find some sugar. Cost more than a night with a top Nogales whore, but I bought it anyway. I'll take your part of the grub cost out of your share of the mustang money."

"Bring any whiskey?" Brubs asked hopefully.

The mustanger shook his head as he stripped

the saddle from his roan. "Nope. I need both you younkers sober until we get a mess of horses caught and delivered."

Willoughby had already unloaded the mule and was rummaging through the packs. Brubs made no offer to lend a hand, even though his belly was growling again. "Find any horse sign, Stump?"

"Found some." Stump shouldered his bedroll and rifle. The two strode toward the camp fire. "About twelve miles west of here. Ten of them running together, all long twos or three-year-olds. Still too young and timid to whip a tough old stud off his mares, but they're good horses. How you boys coming with our *manada?*"

"Doin' all the good," Brubs said. "Got 'em near eatin' out of our hands. At least I ain't been kicked or bit for a whole day now."

Stump said, "Good. We'll use this bunch to help catch the young studs. Won't be nearly as much hard work as last time. Shouldn't take more than three, four days. Then we brand 'em and geld them — change their minds from ass to grass, as us old mustangers say. Then you two younkers can top them out and break them to saddle. They'll be worth twenty-five each, on average, once they're green-broke."

Brubs grinned at the prospect of topping out a few broncs. It might cost him some more skin, but it was a lot more fun than swinging that ax. "Dave and me'll have 'em workin' stock, cookin', and tendin' camp in a week."

"Sure," Stump said. "I'm looking forward to some of that entertainment."

Willoughby glanced up as he sorted through the last of the packs. "There's new clothes in this one, Brubs."

"Figured you two could use them," Stump said. "You're both looking a bit tattered."

"Aw, Stump," Brubs fussed, "what'd you go and waste good money on britches for? You could of bought some good whiskey with them coins."

Stump waved a hand. "I'm tired of looking at your butt, for one thing. It's been hanging out and shining like a full moon since that blood bay chewed your pants off."

Brubs tried to look around at his backside. "It has been a mite drafty, now you mention it. I expect you're gonna tell me to take a bath, too?"

Stump's nose wrinkled. "You're getting a bit ripe, sure enough. Standing downwind from you will make a man's eyes water."

Brubs sighed in resignation. "All right. Anything to stop your bellyachin', you old mossback. But, hell, it's too early in the season for any bath. Ain't September yet."

"Willoughby," Stump said, "if you'll whip up some supper we'll turn in early. We got to move camp and our mares come first light." He reached into a saddlebag. "Almost forgot, McCallan — I brought you these." He tossed a pair of thick leather gloves into Brubs's lap.

Brubs stared at the gloves for a few seconds,

then lifted a wary gaze at the mustanger. "I'm half scared to ask, you old buzzard, but what do I need these for?"

Stump said, "Where we're going there ain't any box canyons handy. Thought you might like to have them while you're building a catch pen in the middle of a mesquite thicket."

Brubs groaned aloud. "Why me? Ain't it Dave's turn on that damn ax?"

"You earned the right, son," Stump said with a grin. "You're getting downright good at it. Besides that, you're learning a trade for when you get tired of chousing mustangs."

"A trade?"

Stump nodded. "Man can make a fair living building fence."

SEVEN

Brubs McCallan crossed his forearms over the top rail of the corral he had built and grinned in satisfaction as he studied the mustangs inside the enclosure.

The catch had been a lot easier this time. Stump and Willoughby had walked the band of young stallions for three days while Brubs labored over the corral and wings of the trap. Then they had brought out the mares as bait. The young studs had been cautious at first, but within an hour they had realized there was no tough old stallion waiting to skin their hides and trotted eagerly into the herd. From then it was just a matter of pointing the whole cavvy in the right direction. The brown mare walked into the catch pen like she expected a crib full of corn to be waiting.

That had been a week ago. The next day Brubs and Willoughby roped the young studs, Dave catching them around the necks and Brubs by the front feet, pulled them down, tied them, and let Stump Hankins go to work with knife and branding iron. Now they had a dozen newly gelded, and considerably more docile, horses on their hands. The new horses were young and fit and healed quickly from the operation.

"Ready to play with some broncs, McCallan?" Stump said from the saddle atop the big roan.

"Never been readier." Brubs felt the tingle of anticipation in his forearms. Nothing short of that redhead up in Denton stirred as much excitement in his gut. Forking a raw bronc was the one thing he did best. Not counting the redhead. "You pen 'em, I skin 'em." Brubs glanced at Willoughby standing an arm's length away. "Grab your rig, partner. We're finally gonna have us some *real* fun."

Willoughby hesitated, a frown on his face.

"What's the matter, amigo? Nothin' like ridin' the rough string to stoke the fire under a cowboy's skillet."

"I've never done anything like this," Willoughby said solemnly. He sounded worried.

Brubs stared at Dave, incredulous. "I thought you told me you growed up around horses. You mean to say you ain't never topped out a bronc?"

"No," Willoughby said with a shake of his head. "Father always bought horses that had already been gentled. I've never been on a wild horse."

"Damn, son," Brubs said with a snort, "I can't make no real, genuine Texan out of a Yankee what can't ride broncs. Think that's a state law or somethin'. Grab your rig and I'll learn you how to do it."

Willoughby's face seemed a bit pale. "I don't

143

know," he said warily. "It looks like it might be rather dangerous."

Brubs shrugged and picked up his saddle and hackamore. "Ain't nothin' to it. You just watch old Brubs McCallan and you'll learn quick how to handle broncs."

Stump Hankins stepped down, tightened the cinch on Choctaw, then remounted and shook out a loop. "Open the gate, Willoughby." He studied the new horses as he waited for the bars to slide open. "I reckon that grulla with the black stockings would be the one to start on, McCallan. Been watching him move. Quick as a cat. Got the makings of a fine rope horse, worth maybe forty, fifty dollars."

Brubs ran a practiced eye over the grulla. He was a little horse, barely fourteen hands tall, and wouldn't weigh nine hundred pounds soaking wet. Despite his size and the almost dainty hooves, the grulla's conformation was good; clean head, intelligent eyes set wide apart, straight legs, a deep girth and hindquarters wider and more heavily muscled than most mustangs.

"Whatever suits you," Brubs said. "They all got hair." He followed the big roan through the gate and dropped his saddle at the base of a stout snubbing post he had planted a few yards from the fence. He knelt to tighten the straps of his spurs as Stump eased his way into the herd.

Stump's loop wasn't much bigger than the grulla's head, but the old mustanger knew how to handle a rope. He fit the loop just behind the throatlatch on the first throw, whipped the slack, and dallied. The grulla bolted, hit the end of the rope, and almost went down as the jolt yanked his head around. He sat back on his haunches and fought the rope, but the wiry, little mouse-colored mustang was no match for the power of the big, rawboned Choctaw. After a couple of minutes, the grulla quit fighting and stood, nostrils flared and eyes walled in fright.

Brubs stepped back as Stump eased the grulla to the snubbing post. The mustanger undallied his rope and tossed a couple of half hitches around the post, then grinned at Brubs. "He's all yours, McCallan. I'm mighty anxious to see your technique."

"It's sweeter'n a fine-tuned fiddle," Brubs said confidently. He untied the grimy bandanna from his neck, slipped the hackamore over his shoulder, put a hand on the rope, and started talking softly as he eased toward the grulla.

The mustang squealed and lunged back against the rope. The fight didn't last long. The noose around his neck quickly choked off the grulla's wind. The horse took a half step forward to relieve the strangling and stood, muscles quivering. Brubs worked his way down the rope to the mustang's head.

"Easy now, son," Brubs muttered softly. He reached out and stroked a hand along the mustang's neck. The horse walled his eyes wider, but didn't try to bite or kick. "You'll be a good one, little feller," Brubs said almost in the horse's ear. "All we got to do is make sure we know who's boss." He kept his movements slow and deliberate as he slipped the bandanna up behind the mustang's ears, then let it drop down until it covered the horse's eyes. Brubs tied it off with a quick knot. The grulla stood quivering, but with its eyes covered it didn't try to fight as Brubs slipped the hackamore onto the horse's head and secured it in place. Brubs lifted the saddle and eased it onto the grulla's back. The horse flinched, hide quivering, at the unaccustomed weight and feel of the saddle. "Easy now," Brubs said. "We done got past the hard part."

He eased the catch rope from around the mustang's neck, stepped into the saddle, turned his toes out, and took a measured grip on the hackamore rein. He clamped his right hand onto the saddle horn and glanced at Stump standing nearby. "I reckon we're ready," he said.

Stump strode to the horse and whipped the bandanna free.

The grulla stood for a moment, confused. Brubs could feel the fear in the quaking muscles of the little mustang. He touched his spurs to the horse's ribs.

The mustang took a couple of mincing steps — then squalled, bogged its head, and fell apart.

Brubs whooped in exuberance as the mustang bucked, its jumps high and floating. Brubs sat the saddle with ease, his spurs raking the mustang's shoulder from neck to saddle girth, legs working in rhythm with the horse's high, twisting jumps.

Then the mustang got dirty.

His fifth jump wasn't high and floating; it was a short, bone-jarring hop on stiff front legs, followed by a choppy half spin to the left. Brubs felt a boot slip in the stirrup. The high cantle of his saddle whopped against his butt. The mustang broke wind, pitching low and hard, head jerking first to one side and then the other. The grulla bucked toward the fence, then went high in the air, kicked its back legs to the right and threw its head and forelegs left. It felt to Brubs as if the horse's belly was turned straight up. He lost the right stirrup, then the left. The cantle swatted him on the butt as the grulla dropped its left shoulder.

Brubs sailed over the horse's neck and crashed against the top rail of the fence. His ribs whacked against the wood a split second before his head cracked against the top of a post. A flash of white light shot through his skull. A flailing hoof cracked against a rail near Brubs's head as the mustang spun away and kicked. Brubs bounced off the rail and tumbled to the hard corral earth.

Brubs lay for a moment, stunned and gasping for air, the sound of the pitching grulla's squeals and grunts faint in his ears. Then Willoughby was at his side.

"Are you all right, Brubs?"

Brubs shook his head to clear the cobwebs

and put a hand to an ear. It came away with a smear of blood on the palm. "What damn fool," Brubs gasped, "put that damn fence right square in my way like that?"

Stump sauntered over and stared down at Brubs. "Thought you said you could ride anything with horsehair on it, McCallan," he said.

Brubs let Willoughby help him to his feet and stood, woozy, his ears ringing. His ribs stabbed a sharp pain through his chest with every gasp for air. "That little . . . sumbitch . . . can sure 'nuff pitch," Brubs finally gasped.

"Noticed that about grullas a long time ago," Stump said casually. "Never saw one that couldn't pitch hard enough to sling sweat, snot, and bronc riders over a half acre. Going to be a good horse, that one. Quicker than I thought he was." Stump peered into Brubs's eyes for a moment. "I reckon you're not hurt much. Just got a little scab over your ear."

Brubs felt Willoughby's hand press against his rib cage and winced. "Stump, he could be hurt inside." Dave's tone was a mix of alarm and concern.

Stump ignored Willoughby's worry. "McCallan, I thought you were a rough-string rider." He sighed heavily. "I guess me and Dave are going to have to top this bunch off."

"Now, wait a minute!" Willoughby's voice held a fresh note of alarm. "You can't expect —"

"Shut up, Dave," Brubs interrupted. "That

148

little mousy son of a bitch done made me mad."
He jabbed a finger at Stump Hankins. The second knuckle of the finger had a freshly skinned spot on it. "You old mossback, I'll show you somethin' about rough strings! You catch that grulla for me. Scrawny little bastard can't do that again."

He could.

He did. Twice more.

Brubs hit the ground for the third time, rolled in the dust, and heaved himself up on his elbows with an effort. His ribs hurt like the blazes, his right knee pained when he moved, and his head throbbed like an Apache drummer with a belly full of peyote. "This ain't," Brubs muttered to himself, "one of my bluebird days."

Stump hadn't even bothered to dismount this time. He trotted Choctaw up to Brubs's side. "Give up, McCallan?"

Brubs gasped for air and glared at the old mustanger. "Hell no, I ain't give up. This here fight's done got personal."

Stump shrugged. "I'll bring him back." He shook his head sadly. "Maybe you aren't much of a bronc rider, McCallan, but you've got sand. I like that in a man."

"Just catch that damn horse, you old badger. I'll tell you when I'm whipped."

Brubs McCallan dragged himself awake and immediately wished he hadn't.

He lay moaning in his blankets, wondering if

any part of his battered body still worked, and mumbled a steady stream of oaths. He was reasonably sure he had a cracked rib; his right hip popped when he moved, and if there was a spot on him that wasn't skinned he didn't know where it was. His butt was black-and-blue from the pounding it had taken the last three days. But he had finally ridden the damn grulla to a standstill.

After the grulla the rest of them seemed easy. Half the new string didn't even try to pitch.

"Good morning, sunshine," Dave Willoughby said cheerfully from the camp fire, "you seem to be in fine fettle. Coffee's ready."

Brubs sat up stiffly, reached for his boots, and looked groggily around the camp. "Where's that gray-bearded old persimmon-eater?"

The grin faded from Willoughby's face. "Stump rode out last night, only a bit after sundown. He looked worried."

"Humph," Brubs grunted. "Prob'ly afraid he wouldn't get back in time to see one of them damn broncs stomp me to pieces today."

Willoughby poured a cup of coffee and handed it to Brubs. "I don't think that was what was on Stump's mind," he said. "I saw him take an extra handful of cartridges from the pack before he rode out. When I asked him if anything was wrong, he just sort of looked at me with this strange expression on his face — a frightening kind of look — and rode off."

Brubs sipped at the coffee, winced, and ran

his tongue across a day-old cut on his swollen lip. The cut had been put there when a mustang tossed its head just as he was about to put on the hackamore. "If he's gone huntin' more mustangs like this last bunch, I'm climbin' his tree," Brubs said. "Well, amigo, if you'll dish up one of those special house breakfasts, we'll go play with some half-broke horses."

Willoughby slid the skillet over the camp fire coals. "Do you think that grulla will pitch today?"

"Nah," Brubs said. "Mouse and me got us a understandin' now. If he don't pitch, I don't shoot him."

Stump Hankins rode in at sunset, frown lines deep in his weathered face. He did not speak as he stripped the saddle from the roan, strode into camp, and sat on his bedroll, the Sharps cradled in the crook of an arm.

Willoughby cast a quick, questioning glance at Brubs. The old mustanger was never far from the big-bore rifle, but he seldom sat holding it like that.

"Got troubles, Stump?" Brubs finally asked.

Stump nodded as he took the coffee Willoughby handed to him. "I found something out there, boys. Something I don't like all that much." He sipped at the coffee and stared at the fire in silence for several minutes.

Finally, Brubs couldn't stand it any longer. "You goin' to let us in on the secret sometime in the next couple of months?"

Stump glared over the edge of his tin cup at Brubs. "I was getting to that, McCallan. Spotted a camp fire a few nights back. It got to eating at me, so I went looking last night. What I found was man-sign. Twelve men. About five miles west."

Brubs's eyebrows went up. "Cherry Cows?"

"Not Apaches." Stump swigged at the scalding coffee. "Mexicans."

"Vaqueros?"

Stump's frown deepened until his bushy eyebrows all but met. "No." He set the coffee cup at his side. His hand stroked the scarred fore stock of the Sharps. "I'm going to lay it straight out for you, boys." Stump's voice took on a hard edge. "I recognized the tracks of one of those horses. Belongs to a pepperbelly son of a bitch named Gilberto Delgado from down in Chihuahua."

"I gather," Willoughby said solemnly, "that this Delgado is no particular friend of yours?"

Stump's tone turned even colder. "Delgado and me have been trying to kill each other for nigh onto ten years now. I damn near nailed him winter before last." Stump snorted in disgust. "I still don't know how I missed that shot by that much. Wasn't more than a couple hundred yards. Creased his ribs instead of busting him between the shoulder blades." Stump fell silent, staring into the fire, the look in his gray eyes hard and intense.

"Stump," Willoughby finally said, "would it be out of line for me to ask the cause of the trouble between you and this Delgado?"

For a few moments it seemed the old mustanger wasn't going to answer. Then he cleared his throat. "That bastard's bunch of bandits killed my boy. We were trailing a herd of mustangs north of Laredo when Delgado's gang bushwhacked us. They shot Sonny. Got a slug in me, left me for dead. Stole our horses." Moisture glistened at the corners of Stump's eyes. "He was a good boy, Sonny. Wasn't but eighteen when he died. The only child Maria and I ever had."

Brubs squirmed in awkward silence. He had never been all that good with words when it came to trying to comfort someone who had suffered a personal and painful loss.

"I'm truly sorry to hear that, Stump," Willoughby finally said. "My sincere condolences. I never heard you mention having a family before. Where is Maria now?"

Stump's shoulders seemed to slump even more. "She's dead, too. Grieved herself to death over Sonny, near as I could tell. I buried her at LaQuesta, little village down in the Big Bend three day's ride west of Laredo. We had a house there. Wasn't but a three-room shack, but it was the best home a man could ever ask for." He sighed heavily, the memories still obviously painful. "Damn, but I did so love that boy and that woman."

Brubs picked up a stick and traced idle patterns into the dirt, still unable to find the right words. Sometimes there just weren't any. Even Dave, with all his Latin lingo and philosophy learning, seemed at a loss.

After a long time, Stump squared his shoulders and said, "Boys, Delgado won't give you any more chance than he gave Sonny if you're riding with me. If you two want to saddle up and ride out now, it sure won't lower my opinion of you one damned bit. I got a few dollars you can have for traveling money. There's no need to take a chance on getting yourselves killed on my account."

Brubs finally stirred. "I reckon we'll stick, Stump. We're partners now, the three of us."

Willoughby cast a quick, worried look at Brubs, then nodded to Stump. "Brubs is right for once," he said, his voice soft. "You're a good man to ride with. We'll stay."

Stump's expression softened again for a few heartbeats. "I figured you two greenhorns had plenty of *cojones* under those flat bellies. I'm obliged to you." He reached into a shirt pocket and handed Dave a folded piece of paper.

"What's this?" Willoughby asked.

"My last will and testament," Stump said. "In case Delgado gets me before I get him, should it come to that. I have no living relatives and not very many friends. You boys are about as close as I have to family. So I want you to have my horses, the brand, and the place in LaQuesta if you want them. There's a couple of sections of land goes with the house and a few dollars hid in a coffee can under a corner brick of the fireplace. All I ask is that you tend Sonny and Maria's graves a couple of times a year."

"Stump, I don't —"

"Let me finish, Willoughby," Stump interrupted. "If you happen to get out of here with the horses and I don't, trail the cavvy to a man name of Bass Jernigan. Runs the BJ brand over west of Goliad. Bass is a good man. He'll give you a fair price and won't niggle you over a few strange brands."

Stump paused to stoke his pipe, then continued. "Now, I don't want you boys to get in my personal shooting war. Delgado's got some of the toughest men in Mexico riding with him. Don't try to buck that bunch." He struck a match, fired his pipe, and squinted through the smoke at the two younger men. "If guns start going off, you two put the steel to your horses and get the hell away if you can. But until we know nothing's going to happen, we all ride with both eyes open and a cartridge in the chamber."

Dave Willoughby sat astride his leggy Tennessee black and watched as Brubs McCallan stripped the saddle from the sweaty little mouse-colored mustang. The grulla shook its head, then nuzzled Brubs's shoulder as the stocky Texan removed the hackamore. Brubs scratched the horse behind the ear before walking back toward Dave.

"It appears that you and Mouse have become fast friends in the last few days, Brubs," Willoughby said. "I must say it's an impressive transformation since the first time the two of you met."

Brubs turned to stare at the grulla. Mouse sniffed at a bare spot in the corral, then lay down in the sand. The grulla's hooves flailed as he dusted himself, rolling from one side to the other. "Yeah," Brubs said laconically. "Gettin' to be a bigger pest than a hungry dog, but at least he's blowin' friendly snot and slobbers on me now. He's gonna make a top horse. Might just decide to keep him."

Willoughby straightened in the saddle and let his gaze drift over as much of the Mustang Mesa countryside as he could see. The catch pen was built on the east side of a shallow basin. From the corral a man had only a limited view of the land. It wasn't nearly as comfortable a feeling to Willoughby now as it had been when they had first made camp.

"Where's Stump at?"

Willoughby waved a hand toward the western edge of the basin. "Out there, somewhere. Still scouting for Delgado's bunch. He said if we heard shots, we would know he found them and to get out fast." His hand unconsciously dropped to the stock of the Winchester in his saddle boot.

"Aw, relax, partner," Brubs said. "If them Mexes was still out there Stump would of found 'em by now, or we'd have cut sign ourselves." He lugged the saddle to where his sorrel stood hitched to a corral rail, half dozing, and started to saddle up. "I reckon this Delgado ain't goin' to amount to a quail fart in a whirlwind, Dave." He settled a thick horsehair pad carefully on the sorrel's back, swung the saddle into place, and reached under the horse's belly for the cinches. "Anyhow, these new horses is green-broke and herd-tame now. Stump says we'll start trailin' 'em to Goliad first light tomorrow." He pulled the cinches tight, bringing a resigned sigh from the sorrel.

"I'm not exactly disheartened at that news," Willoughby said. "I will be more than a bit relieved to say good-bye to Mustang Mesa. A man could get killed out here."

Brubs said, "It ain't such a bad place. We had us some fun here. Only drawback is there ain't a woman or a whiskey bottle for more'n fifty miles." His face brightened. "But they got some of each in Goliad, and I got enough skin growed back to use 'em both." He retrieved his rifle from the corral post it leaned against, levered the action open a crack to make sure a cartridge was chambered, then mounted and slid the weapon into its scabbard.

As they rode the fifty yards to camp, Willoughby noticed that Brubs's gaze frequently swept the low ridges beyond the shallow basin.

Dave couldn't shake the feeling that Brubs was worried, despite all his talk to the contrary. And when Brubs McCallan got worried, any sane man came down with a lingering bellyache.

Stump Hankins rode in a half hour before sundown, his thick shoulders slumped in weariness. Willoughby fussed over the bubbling stew pot on the coals and wondered how the old man could have such stamina. He knew Stump hadn't slept more than six hours over the last three days.

"See anything, Stump?" Brubs's voice was soft against the early evening air.

"Cut some day-old sign," Stump said as he stripped the saddle from the big roan. "Nothing fresher."

"Do you suppose they pulled out?" Willoughby asked hopefully. "Maybe they never saw us."

Stump flexed his shoulders and stared toward the lowering sun, his Sharps rifle in hand. "The son of a bitch is out there. I can feel him."

The knot in Willoughby's gut tightened. It was a feeling almost forgotten, the grinding tension of waiting and wondering that had been with him from one battlefield to another. It was a part of war, the waiting — a part that was sometimes as hard on a man's nerves as the battle itself.

Stump finally turned back to the fire, his weathered face dark and foreboding. A coyote yelped in the distance, greeting the sunset. A second coyote, then a third, yipped replies. A pair of Mexican jays squawked and quarreled over a roosting site in the brush nearby. The animal sounds were normally soothing to Willoughby, but not this night.

"We'd best stand watch again tonight, boys," Stump said. "I'll take first watch, McCallan the second. Willoughby, you stand third. That'll be the darkest part of the night, and you've got the best night vision. We'll start the cavvy toward Goliad at first light."

Dave Willoughby sighed in relief as the sun poked its top rim above the eastern sky.

It had been, he admitted to himself, one of the most nerve-racking nights he had spent since the war.

At his watch post on the highest point of the east side of the shallow basin, he had started at every real or imagined movement in the darkness broken only by faint starlight. Once he had almost fired a shot at a sudden rustle in the mesquite nearby, but the movement had only been the scuttle of a field mouse.

He had neither seen nor heard any indication that men were about. There were no points of light marking a camp fire, no warning nickers or sudden movements among the mustangs corralled below or from the black gelding tied to a stubby mesquite at his side. It had been quiet. Almost too quiet.

Willoughby stood, stretched the tension of

waiting and watching from his shoulders, and surveyed Mustang Mesa for a final time. The only movement in the soft wash of new dawn light was the wary slink of a hunting coyote two hundred yards away.

He turned toward the camp. Stump and Brubs were already set to move out, pack mules loaded with their remaining supplies. Stump's roan and Brubs's sorrel were saddled and waiting at the picket line. Most of the packing had been done the night before. Willoughby's bedroll, canteen, and saddlebags were strapped in place on the black. That was fine with Dave. The sooner they left Mustang Mesa, the more comfortable he would feel.

He mounted, sheathed his rifle, and kneed the black toward camp. Stump and Brubs were already at the horse corral by the time he trotted up.

"See anything?" Stump asked.

Willoughby shook his head. "All quiet."

Stump pulled the final pole of the makeshift corral gate free and swung aboard Choctaw. "Let's trail some horses, boys," he said. "Willoughby, you take the point. McCallan and I will ease the cavvy out — *son of a bitch!*"

Stump sat stiff in the saddle, staring toward the western rim of the basin.

Willoughby glanced up and felt his heart skip a beat.

A dozen mounted men were skylined on the rim, rifles and handguns drawn.

EIGHT

"Delgado!" Stump Hankins barked the name like a curse.

Dave Willoughby felt the cold fist of dread and fear clamp around his gut. "Stump," he said, "I never saw —"

"Doesn't matter now, son." Hankins's tone was brittle and cold. He stared toward the ridge, a blood vessel throbbing in his temple.

Willoughby heard the whisper of metal against leather as Brubs McCallan shucked his rifle from the saddle scabbard, cocked the hammer, and dismounted. "Your call, Stump," Brubs said calmly as he knelt and shouldered the weapon. "We can take a few of 'em down from here."

Stump's gaze never moved from the ridge. "No. You boys light a shuck. Get the hell out of here while you can, like I told you."

Willoughby pulled his own rifle. He clutched the metal of the receiver hard to stop the tremble that had started in his suddenly chilled fingers. "What about you, Stump?"

"It stops here. One way or another." Stump's hand dropped to the butt of the handgun at his belt. "This time, by God, one of us doesn't ride off."

"Stump, you can't take that bunch on by

yourself," Willoughby pleaded. "They'll cut you down cold!"

Stump Hankins finally tore his gaze from the line of mounted men and glared hard at Willoughby. "If I get that pepperbelly son of a bitch it'll be a fair trade." The expression in Stump's slitted gray eyes was wild, almost insane. Willoughby had seen the look before, the blazing stare in the eyes of soldiers formed up for an attack, driven by hate beyond the fear of death.

"I ain't giving up them horses without no fight," Brubs said, his voice tight. "I got too many pieces of me invested in them animals."

"To hell with the horses, McCallan," Stump snapped. "You can get more. Mount up, damn your stubborn soul, and light a shuck out of here. *Now!*" The old mustanger drew and cocked his handgun. "All hell's fixing to break loose."

"Stump, please —"

"Delgado, you son of a bitch!" Stump Hankins's challenge boomed over the shallow basin, drowning Willoughby's plea. "Your greaser ass is mine now!" The old mustanger rammed spurs to the big roan. Choctaw was in a dead run, charging toward the middle of the line of gunmen, before Brubs or Willoughby could react.

The roan thundered toward the ridge. Willoughby's heart skidded as powder smoke billowed from a half dozen rifles a split second before the crack of muzzle blasts rolled over the mesa. Stump's body jerked at the impact of lead, but the old man stayed in the saddle. A slug ricocheted past Willoughby's ear. He could only sit and watch, mesmerized, as Stump's roan closed to within forty yards, then thirty, of the blazing guns on the ridge. Stump's handgun barked; a tall man on a gray horse lurched and almost fell from the saddle.

The crack of Brubs's rifle jarred Willoughby back to reality. One of the men kneeling on the ridge dove for the cover of a juniper bush. Willoughby wheeled the black a half turn to the right and slapped a quick, unaimed shot toward the ridge. Through the powder smoke he saw Stump tumble over the rump of the roan beneath the crackle of gunfire. Willoughby felt a quick stab of pain and emptiness in his gut as the old mustanger's body fell beside a mesquite, rolled a couple of times, and lay still. Dave slapped two more quick rounds toward the ridge.

"Mount up, Brubs!" Willoughby yelled. A slug plucked at his shirt, another kicked dust near the black's front feet. A half dozen riders quirted horses down the ridge toward the corral. "We can't help Stump now! We've got to get out of here!" He took a split second to steady his aim and fired at one of the approaching horsemen as Brubs swung into the saddle. The man's horse stumbled and went down.

Willoughby wheeled the black and drove the spurs home. The gelding was in a dead run within two jumps. A slug buzzed past Dave's ear, another hummed over his head. Then Brubs was alongside Willoughby, leaning over the neck of the wide-eyed sorrel. The big black and the sorrel raced stride for stride through the mesquite and cactus; the gunfire behind them slowed, then stopped. Willoughby glanced over his shoulder as his black topped the east lip of the basin.

Four riders on wiry Spanish horses spurred past the corral in pursuit of the fleeing mustangers. Others reined in, already slipping the gate poles to move the horse herd out. Willoughby knew it would be a horse race now, with lead slugs as the stakes.

"Thataway!" Brubs yelled, jabbing the muzzle of his rifle toward a broken range of badlands at the base of the peak two miles away.

In the first mile Brubs and Willoughby gained a hundred yards on the bandits, the big American-bred horses gobbling up the ground with their longer strides. But Willoughby soon felt the black weaken, its breathing more labored by the yard. He glanced back again. The little Spanish ponies were gaining on them now, with their greater stamina and wind. He knew it was only a matter of time until the black and sorrel gave out. They were losing the race.

A hundred yards ahead the trail dipped past a mesquite clump and a jumble of small boulders at the edge of a shallow creek. Brubs pointed toward the dip in the trail. As the two men neared the rocks and mesquite, Brubs yelled, "Go on, Dave! I'll slow 'em down a tad!"

"Brubs —"

"Shut up and git!" Brubs yelled. He yanked his sorrel to an abrupt stop. Willoughby glanced back as Brubs leapt from the saddle and ducked behind the rocks. Delgado's men were less than two hundred yards behind and closing fast.

Willoughby hauled back on the reins as the black jumped the shallow groove of the creek bed. He managed to check the winded gelding just beyond the far creek bank. He scrambled from the saddle and flopped on his belly at the lip of the creek, breathing hard, Winchester tucked against his shoulder.

The first of the four pursuers quirted his horse to within fifty yards of the rockfall. Brubs's rifle barked. The bandit twitched, slumped over his horse's neck, then fell. A second man less than ten yards back yelped, grabbed at a leg, and reined aside at Brubs's second shot. Then the third man, handgun drawn, was thundering down on Brubs. Willoughby forced himself to wait a heartbeat to be sure of his aim and stroked the trigger.

The bandit's handgun blasted almost in Brubs's face as Willoughby's .44-40 slug hammered him from the saddle. The fourth rider yanked his horse into a tight turn and spurred hard, trying to flee the ambush. Willoughby levered in a fresh round, steadied his aim, and fired. For an instant he thought he had missed. Then the rider sagged, slid from the saddle, hit the ground, rolled, and lay still. Gravel stung Willoughby's cheek a split second before he heard the flat bark of a handgun. The bandit Brubs had hit in the leg had wheeled his horse back toward the fight. Willoughby twisted, brought his Winchester into line, squeezed the trigger — and heard the dull click as the hammer fell on an empty chamber. He braced himself for the bullet shock as the bandit bore down on him, pistol muzzle leveled.

The Mexican's handgun spun in the air; the man lifted from the saddle as if hit by a fist, seemed to hang for a moment in midair, then fell as the crack of Brubs's rifle reached Dave's ears. Willoughby knew the man was dead before he hit the ground. He had seen head shots before.

Willoughby let his breath out in a long sigh and glanced at the stocky man beside the rocks. Brubs knelt on one knee, rifle in hand. He raised a hand to his neck, then all but ripped the bandanna from his throat and threw it down. A wisp of smoke drifted from the charred cloth.

Willoughby scrambled to his feet and sprinted to Brubs's side. "Are you all right, Brubs? Are you hit?"

Brubs's normally ruddy face was pale above a smear of blood at his neck. "Damn if you ain't makin' a livin' out of askin' me if I'm all right. I'm standin' here, which like not to have been the case." He jabbed a thumb toward the body a few feet away. "That Mex near shot me square

166

in the face. Sure got my ear to ringin'. I ain't hearin' so good out of that side."

"Let's have a look," Willoughby said. His fingers shook as he plucked away a few scorched threads stuck to the blood on Brubs's neck and peered at the wound. "It appears that you have a shallow bullet crease and a bit of a powder burn. The eardrum doesn't appear to be broken. Nothing serious, if that neck wound doesn't get infected. I've seen blood poisoning set in from less."

Brubs snorted. "You got a funny way of bringin' comfort to a man, Dave Willoughby. Always got to turn good news into bad. I'd of been a sight happier if you'd shot that Mex just a hair quicker."

"Wanted to make sure of my shot," Willoughby said by way of apology. "Speaking of which — and not that I'm complaining, mind you — but why did you chance a head shot on that man who was about to kill me?"

Brubs raised a quizzical eyebrow. "Head shot? Amigo, I was tryin' to hit the *horse*." He shrugged. "Guess it don't matter. It all worked out." He waved a hand. "These jaspers all dead?"

A quick check showed that they were — or would be, in a few minutes.

Brubs paused long enough to strip a neckerchief from one of the bodies and yank a Colt .45 from the man's holster. "Their horses get away?"

"All four," Willoughby said. He was still edgy even though the raw fear had eased a bit. His gaze flicked about the countryside. "They bolted back the way they came."

Brubs tucked the captured gun under his belt. "Guess old Delgado'll know soon enough what happened to his hired hands."

"That thought has crossed my mind, too," Willoughby said. "Perhaps we should put a few miles between ourselves and Delgado's bunch? He might be a bit angry with us."

Brubs sniffed at the liberated bandanna. "Wouldn't surprise me a bit if there's cooties in this thing," he said. He draped it around his neck anyway, then stared at Willoughby. "Son, you don't look so good. Sorta peaked, in fact. A touch green around the gills. You didn't stop no lead, did you?"

Willoughby suppressed a shudder. "No. It's just that — well, I never killed a man before."

"Didn't you say you was in the artillery?"

"Yes."

"Then this ain't the first time you killed somebody. It's just the first time you done it close up and friendly."

Willoughby felt the cold sweat bead on his forehead. "This is — different, somehow."

Brubs shrugged. "I reckon. Killin' a man eyeball-to-eyeball does twang the nerves a bit. But hell, partner. These wasn't men. They was Mexican bandits." He reached into his saddlebag, produced a box of cartridges, and casually began reloading his rifle.

The chill on Willoughby's forehead crept down into his belly. "Brubs, we'd better get a move on. Delgado's band could come over that hill any minute. I would be considerably more comfortable about thirty miles east of here."

Brubs toed the stirrup and swung aboard. "Then don't just stand there all pale and sweaty, partner. I better get you busy before you throw up on me. Fork that black. Might want to reload that Winchester first." He waited until Willoughby retrieved his gelding and swung into the saddle, then leaned over and tucked the dead man's pistol into Dave's saddlebag. "Can't never tell when you might need a hideout gun," Brubs said. "Let's move out." He reined his sorrel toward the east.

They had ridden in silence for a mile, moving at a stiff trot, before Brubs abruptly kneed his horse toward the north.

Willoughby pulled his black to a stop. "What are you doing?"

"We ain't goin' no farther east, partner."

Willoughby felt the chill deepen. "I'm almost afraid to ask, but what, precisely, do you have in mind?"

Brubs's sandy brows were bunched, the expression in the deep brown eyes cold. "We're goin' back to the corral. We're goin' to take Stump home and bury him proper." His voice seemed to catch in his throat. "I liked that cantankerous old badger. I reckon it's the least we can do, put him beside his Maria and his boy."

Willoughby raised a hand. "Wait a minute — what about Delgado's band? They'll put so much lead in us we'd sink into solid rock."

"Delgado got what he wanted," Brubs snorted. "He'll be halfway to Mexico with those mustangs by now, I reckon." Brubs cast a challenging glance at Willoughby. "You goin' to give me a hand with Stump?"

Willoughby sighed and touched spurs to the black. "Yes. I suppose we owe him that much. He was a good man."

"If it'll make you feel better," Brubs said, "we'll go roundabout, scout the country some, and make sure Delgado's gone before we go fetch Stump."

The two rode for a full hour before Brubs spoke again. "How come you didn't keep on ridin' back there like I told you?"

Willoughby sighed. "I didn't think it would be right to leave a partner behind to face four-to-one odds."

"Well, you sure ain't much at followin' orders."

Willoughby cast a quick glance at Brubs. "I pulled rank. You were a private, weren't you?"

Brubs turned his head, spat, and winced as the skin of the raw burn stretched. "Yep. Went in a private, come out a private. Damn proud of that record, too."

"I was an officer. A lieutenant."

Brubs's neck colored above the borrowed

neckerchief. "Lordy me, but I can pick 'em. A college boy blue-leg who can't rope, ride the rough string, shoot worth a flip, and near ups his chuck over a simple killin'. Now that much, I can overlook. But a damn army *officer* on top of ever'thing else?" He sighed in mock disgust. "How in the Great Spirit's cactus patch can I make a real, genuine Texan out of that recipe?"

Willoughby fought back a flush of irritation. "Maybe you should just give up on the project."

"Nah. You're gettin' better."

"Better?"

Brubs gestured toward Dave's belt buckle. "This time you didn't pee in your pants."

Stump Hankins was getting ripe, Brubs McCallan had to admit.

He had ridden the better part of the last sixty miles on the upwind side of the body, which was lashed between two drag poles of the makeshift travois that trailed behind Dave Willoughby's black.

Stump had fallen from the travois twice along the rugged trails of the desert mountains northwest of the Pecos River. It was hell's own time wrestling the stiff body back onto the lattice work of ropes and limbs between the drag poles. Willoughby's black didn't like the idea much, either. He still snorted and fought against the load. The first time out the black had boogered something fierce and kicked the body trailing behind his hocks. Brubs figured

171

that didn't matter much to Stump.

Stump was wrapped in a couple of old worn-out blankets, about all Delgado's men had left behind except the body. After Delgado, the Mustang Mesa horse camp looked worse than Georgia after Sherman. The grub was gone. Brubs and Willoughby had been living on growling guts and an occasional rabbit for days. The Mexes had taken all the horses and mules, including Choctaw and Mouse, along with Stump's saddle and weapons. They had even taken the old man's clothes, stripping him down to his underwear. Brubs figured they would have taken it, too, but old Stump's drawers were not spotless clean and had a lot of holes in them, anyway.

Delgado's bunch had even swiped the digging tools. Brubs had a hard time figuring that. A man who would steal something that raised blisters must be a couple of aces short of a full deck as far as Brubs was concerned.

Brubs had been stewing over the loss of the horses all during the week it took to strap Stump to the drag and hunt up LaQuesta. The last part hadn't been any easier than the first part.

LaQuesta wouldn't have been nearly as hard to find if it had been bigger, Brubs thought, as he kneed his sorrel toward what would have been the main street if the village had had streets.

LaQuesta lay in the bowl of a valley between dry mountains laced by deep canyons studded with rocks, thick with mesquite and cactus but thin on most everything else. At least LaQuesta had water and grass. Brubs figured that was all that kept the town alive. A small stream wound its way from north to south down the valley and trickled east of the dozen adobe shacks, half of them little more than crumbled walls and fallen roof timbers, that made up LaQuesta. A stone-wall well stood in the center of the sun-baked buildings, a leaky horse trough beside the well. The adobes were scattered about haphazardly as if some giant hand had tossed them like dice and let them stay where they fell.

A scraggly rooster scratched in the dirt beside the first house at the edge of the village as Brubs and Dave rode past. The rooster found a kernel of corn or something, clucked to alert his harem to the find, then pounced on the morsel and ate it just before the hens got there. Brubs thought that was a pretty mean way to treat females, but chickens were a sight dumber than men. Maybe.

A Mexican woman as broad as she was tall and dressed in little more than rags squatted behind a charcoal pit outside one hovel and stared in silent suspicion at the two Anglo intruders. A yellow cur dog, its ribs showing beneath skin that was missing several patches of hair, trotted out from behind a building, growled at the intruders, then apparently decided it was too hot to bother with them and slunk from sight.

Two brown-skinned kids rolling an iron wagon wheel hoop with a stick were about the only signs of energetic life in LaQuesta. The kids stopped playing to stare at the gringos dragging the stinking bundle. Brubs had the feeling LaQuesta hadn't seen a stranger in years.

Brubs's enthusiasm for LaQuesta perked up considerably as they neared the only structure of any size, a run-down, two-story adobe across from the well. He knew at a glance what the building was, and breathed a deep sigh of gratitude. Brubs McCallan could smell a cantina from ten miles away even when his mouth didn't feel like the inside of a cornshuck mattress from a long, dry trail.

He kneed his sorrel toward the sagging hitch rail in front of the cantina. Up close he could make out the faded hand-lettered sign in red paint over the sagging door. The owner didn't spell much better than he did himself, Brubs thought. The lettering read SYMM'S DRY GODDS & SALON.

He figured a "salon" was as good as a saloon if they had beer and whiskey. They could spell it any way they wanted. And if the spirits took offense to "Godds," that was up to them.

"Tell old Stump we're home, amigo," Brubs said casually to Willoughby, "and break out a couple of them fifteen dollars we got stashed back. I'm so thirsty I can't even spit."

Willoughby's brows bunched in a frown. "It's fourteen. And we can't waste money on whiskey. We have barely enough for food."

Brubs grinned and held out a hand, palm up.

"Son, you ought to know by now that whiskey's food, just like beans and biscuits. Only better. We earned us a couple bucks worth of dust-cuttin' medicine."

Willoughby muttered something under his breath, then pulled a couple of coins from his pocket. "Every time you get around liquor, Brubs McCallan, it seems that I wind up in some kind of trouble." He reluctantly handed over the coins. "What about Stump?"

Brubs waved a hand in dismissal. "He's kept this long. He'll keep another half hour." Brubs dismounted, looped the sorrel's reins over the hitch rail, and glanced up at Willoughby. "You comin', or am I gonna have to do everything by myself?"

Willoughby hesitated, then shrugged and stepped down.

The interior of Symm's Dry Godds & Salon smelled of dust, neglect, stale whiskey, and tobacco smoke. It was Brubs's kind of place.

Most of Symm's was devoted to drinking space. The "dry godds" part was limited to one end of the shotgun-style room, a few mostly bare shelves that held a jumble of tinned goods, coffee, and salt, with flour and cornmeal sacks stacked underneath. It looked to Brubs like mice had been into most of the cornmeal. At first he thought the place was deserted, but as his eyes adjusted to the dim light he spotted a man slumped behind the bar, a bottle at his elbow and a half-empty glass in front of him.

"Hey, barkeep," Brubs said, "got any whiskey here?"

The man behind the bar looked up. "Got any money?"

Brubs flashed a quick grin. "More'n the Fort Worth and Denver Railroad. How's about dishin' up a couple shots?"

The man heaved himself from his stool and reached under the stained counter. Up close, Brubs could see that the flesh around the man's eyes was puffy, the nose laced by small pink tracks. A thin fringe of fuzz at the temples accounted for all the hair on the man's head, not counting the wad that stuck out from each ear hole. A sizeable potbelly protruded through a frayed shirt missing a couple of buttons at gut level. It looked to Brubs like the man had downed more whiskey than he sold. Probably played hell with the profits, he figured.

Two glasses, murky with smudged fingerprints, thumped onto the bar. The barkeep sullenly poured a dribble of whiskey into each glass. "That'll be four bits."

Brubs dropped a silver dollar on the bar. "Kind of proud of your whiskey, aren't you, friend?"

Perspiration dotted the pink skin on the man's bald head. "My place. I call the price."

"That your name on the sign out front?"

"Yeah. Symms. Barley Symms. You don't like the price, it ain't but fifty miles to the next saloon."

"Too far for me, I reckon." Brubs tossed back the shot, winced, and sighed. "Worst whiskey I ever drank," he said. "Sure does hit the spot." He glanced at Willoughby, who stood and stared at the grimy glass before him. "You gonna drink that or just study on it?"

Willoughby's upper lip crinkled. "This glass is dirty." He pushed the shot glass away. Brubs grabbed it. "I'll have a bottle of beer, if you please, Mr. Symms."

"God, no!" Brubs blurted. "Don't you dare give that man no beer bottle, Symms. He got hisself a nasty habit of bustin' 'em over my head."

The man behind the counter shrugged. "Got no beer in bottles anyhow. Keg and mugs is all."

"That will suffice," Willoughby said pointedly, "as long as the mug is clean."

Symms lifted an eyebrow. "Pretty picky for a saddle tramp, ain't you?"

"Symms," Brubs said, "you got to make allowance for my partner here. He ain't a real Texan yet. Got some funny ways about him."

Symms scratched his ample belly and turned to slosh a mug in a pan of water and wipe it with a stained towel. He paused to take a pull from his own bottle before filling the mug and thumping it down in front of Willoughby. "Ten cents," he said.

"Take it out of the change we got coming."

"Oh. Yeah." Symms sounded disheartened. Brubs figured the man had never intended to

177

make change, just pocket what was left over. He wasn't overly impressed with Barley Symms.

Willoughby contemplated the foamy beer for a moment, then lifted the mug cautiously, took a tentative sip, and visibly relaxed. "I must admit it's a decent brew."

Symms shrugged. "My woman made it herself. It ought to be aged good. Don't get many paying customers in here since they moved the freight line road north eight, nine years ago. Nothing left in this damn town but Mexicans. Where you boys headed?"

"Here," Brubs said. "We brung Stump Hankins home."

"About time that old coot showed up again," Symms grumbled. "Still owes me two dollars."

Brubs sipped from the shot glass. "Reckon you can just count that a loss, Symms. Stump's dead."

Symms grunted in disgust. "Figures. Anything to beat me out of two bucks. You two kill him?"

"Nope," Brubs said. "He was our mustangin' partner. Mex bandits got 'im. We brung 'im here for buryin'." Brubs downed the last of his whiskey, cast a longing look toward the bottle just out of his reach, and glanced hopefully at Willoughby. He shook his head. Brubs sighed in disappointment.

"Mr. Symms," Willoughby said, "would you please tell us where we might find the Hankins place? We would like to lay Stump to rest beside his family."

Symms jabbed a thumb over his shoulder. "Last house north up the valley. Only one with a barn still standing."

"Is there a preacher in town? We should have a service for Stump. Perhaps the residents of LaQuesta would like to attend."

Symms snorted again. "We ain't had a preacher since the Reverend Duckworth got caught fooling around with Juaquin Andujar's woman ten years back. Juaquin gutted him like a pig." Symms chuckled as if the disembowelment of the preacher were the funniest thing in the world. "Far as Stump's concerned, no need for a service. People in this town wouldn't stir out of their houses if the Virgin Mary was spread-eagled buck naked in the middle of the street." He snorted in disgust. "Damn pepperbellies. Don't hardly buy nothing here anymore. Even make their own rotgut liquor. I used to have a middling good business before the white men all left."

Willoughby finished his beer, wiped a hand across his lips, and pushed away from the bar. "Let's go, Brubs. We have a friend to bury."

"You boys stop back on your way out," Symms said. His words were beginning to slur from the kick of the whiskey. "Cash customers always welcome here."

Willoughby touched his fingers to his hat brim. "We'll be back, Mr. Symms. We have to pick up a few supplies before we leave town. The bandits took everything we had."

Brubs stepped back from the bar and sighed. "Be a damn shame to leave LaQuesta. Nice, peaceful little place. Only thing it needs is a good sportin' house."

"We got one whore," Symms said. "She ain't come downstairs yet, though. Sleeps late."

"Well, glory be," Brubs said, a wide grin spreading over his face. "The Lord's lookin' after us for sure, Brother Dave. What's she charge?"

Symms reached for his private bottle. "Five bucks."

Brubs pursed his lips in a silent whistle. "Pretty expensive for a small-town whore."

Symms lifted the bottle and lowered the contents by two inches. "I own her, too. You don't like the price —"

Brubs cut him off with a wave of the hand. "I know, I know. It ain't but fifty miles to the next whore. Let's go, Dave. We got to get old Stump planted while there's still some meat on his bones."

Brubs McCallan leaned against the top plank of the board fence surrounding the small burial plot and watched as a sweaty Dave Willoughby shoveled dirt over the remains of Stump Hankins.

It wasn't a bad place to spend eternity, Brubs decided, if a man had to go — and everybody did sometime. The plot nestled against the side of a hill, facing the sunset on a jagged mountain range across the valley. The graves of Stump's wife and son were obviously well-tended, free of weeds and rocks and covered with grass. Wild flowers grew along the whitewashed stake fence enclosing the site. All in all, Brubs conceded, a sort of peaceful place.

Stump's cabin sat a hundred yards away beneath the shade of a grove of big cottonwoods along the creek that led toward LaQuesta. A stone well similar to the one in town stood near the back door. A barn considerably bigger than the house sat downstream, flanked by two log corrals. The barn had its own well. A series of split logs, the centers burned out to form a crude trough, delivered water to the corrals. Stump had planned things out pretty well, Brubs decided. This way he didn't have to lug water a bucket a time to the wooden horse troughs in the corrals.

The structures were beginning to show signs of neglect and disuse. The cabin needed a fresh dab of adobe here and there where the hand-made bricks of grass and mud had begun to crumble. A couple of rails were down in the smaller corral, and a support post of the wagon shed attached to the barn leaned precariously to the side. The place needed some work, but not all that much. Nothing that Willoughby couldn't handle, Brubs figured.

Brubs had already ridden out the valley — a tour he made while Willoughby dug Stump's grave — and was impressed with the bequest the old mustanger had made to his new friends. At the north end of the valley a deep natural pool of clear, cool water marked the spring that fed the creek. The valley floor was carpeted in tall, lush grass, a sharp contrast to the generally barren and parched countryside. That was an indication that water lay close beneath the surface.

The entire valley was enclosed. Where the hills did not form a natural barrier, fences of rocks and logs kept livestock from drifting in or out. The fences didn't stop the wild animals, of course. Tracks ranging from tiny field mouse prints to quail, turkey, and deer were thick along the banks of the creek.

Willoughby grunted aloud as he heaved another load of soil over Stump's grave, then leaned on the shovel handle and stared at Brubs. "It wouldn't kill you to do a little of this shoveling yourself, Brubs," Willoughby said as he swabbed a neckerchief across his sweaty brow.

Brubs grinned at Willoughby. "Partner, you're doin' such a fine job there, I'd sure hate to mess it up. Besides, this bullet burn on my neck still smarts something fierce."

Willoughby grimaced. "Brubs McCallan, I know quite well you grow new skin faster than a lizard grows a new tail. That crease is all but healed and you know it. I don't think I've ever met a lazier man than you in my life."

"Lazy?" Brubs squawked, indignant. "If you'll recall, I was the one built all them pens and wings while you was off admirin' your shadow on horseback, happy as a tick on a fat hound, and trailin' mustangs."

Willoughby stared at a palm. "I'm getting a blister."

"Stump used to say blisters was good for a man's soul," Brubs said. "He was a mighty likeable old codger, but he had a few funny ideas in that gray head." Brubs turned his head and spat. "You finish up here and I'll go rustle us up some supper from Stump's cupboard. Be sure and put that shovel back in the barn when you get through."

Willoughby glowered for a moment at Brubs, then turned back to his shoveling.

The cabin's wooden door sagged on one hinge, but the shelves and cabinets inside held tinned goods, a full sack of Arbuckle's coffee, a jar of dried apples, and a half keg of flour that hadn't sprouted weevils yet. There was enough wood in the firebox for a couple of meals. Brubs filled an oak stave water bucket from the well outside. He found Stump's coffeepot, a couple of mugs, a pan, and a skillet.

Brubs had the fireplace going and water heating before Willoughby wandered in, brushing the dirt from his hands and clothes.

"Amigo," Brubs said, "I been doin' some thinkin'."

Willoughby lifted his gaze toward the ceiling. "God help us."

"Old Stump deserved better than gettin' killed

by that son of a bitch Delgado. And speakin' of which —"

"Here it comes," Willoughby interrupted with a visible wince. "I can feel it. The opening gust of the wind of doom."

"The Mex bastard stole our horses to boot," Brubs continued. "Now, that's been gallin' on me ever since Mustang Mesa. I maybe don't show it, partner, but I done got madder'n a wet hen over that. We earned them mustangs with sweat and several chunks of my own personal skin. Besides, I never could abide a damn dishonest horse thief."

Willoughby's eyes narrowed in suspicion. "You'd better not be thinking what I think you're thinking."

"We're gonna go get our horses back, even if we got to track that bandit plumb through Mexico."

Willoughby stared in silence for a moment at the stocky Texan. "Tell me," he finally said warily, "that you're not serious."

"Never been seriouser."

"Brubs McCallan, you are stark, raving mad," Willoughby said incredulously. "In case it's slipped your mind, we killed four of Delgado's men back there. Stump may have gotten a slug into Delgado, too. I doubt seriously that Gilberto Delgado has forgotten that little set of facts. He might even be feeling a bit hostile toward the two of us."

Brubs reached for the coffee and dumped a

handful into the pot. "He ain't the only one hostile. Longer I think on it, the madder I get."

"I suppose you have this all planned out?"

"Sure. Wouldn't of mentioned it otherwise. We just mosey on down into Chihuahua, find Delgado, and steal our ponies back."

"Just like that." Willoughby sighed heavily. "Let it go, Brubs. We may be right back where we started, broke, dirty, tired, and disgusted, but at least we're alive."

Brubs shook his head sadly. "You Yankees just ain't got no ambition."

"No ambition to get killed over a handful of mangy mustangs," Willoughby said. "If those broncs haven't kicked every ounce of brains out of your head, think about this." He held out a hand, index finger extended. "One. There are only two of us. We know Delgado's got at least seven gunmen left. Maybe he has more waiting in Mexico."

"There you go again with that down-in-the-mouth talk, Dave Willoughby. Always tryin' to tell a man somethin' can't be did, 'stead of helpin' him do it." Brubs snorted. "It don't matter if he's got a hundred men. We're just gonna steal them horses back, not shoot every Mexican south of the Rio Grande."

Willoughby ignored him and stuck out another finger. "Two. We don't know where Delgado is." He extended another finger. "Three. Even if we did go after him, neither of us knows the country or speaks the language —"

"I know a little Mex."

"Four. Traveling takes money."

"Stump had forty dollars hid in a tobacco can."

"Five. You've been trying to get me killed since San Antonio. Maybe you truly believe it is your mission in life to see me dead. But not this time. I absolutely, positively, flatly and adamantly refuse to cooperate with you in that mission. And this time, Brubs McCallan, there is no way on God's green earth you can talk me into it."

NINE

Brubs McCallan reined his sorrel to a stop beside a sprawling prickly pear patch, lifted himself in the stirrups and squinted against the glare of a high, hard sun across windblown sand dotted by occasional patches of Spanish dagger and scrub mesquite.

The only movement in the sprawling desert was the shimmer of heat waves and the miniature funnel of a dust devil spinning across the desolate landscape.

Brubs dropped back into the saddle and turned to the man on the black gelding at his side. "Dave Willoughby, you gone and done it again," Brubs said. "Got us smack-dab lost in the middle of the most godforsaken country I ever seen."

"*I* got us lost?" Willoughby sniffed, indignant. "I thought *you* were the expert on Mexico and desert navigation."

"Now, partner, there ain't no need to get your back up like a mad cat about it," Brubs said soothingly. "I reckon it ain't your fault we missed the road to Coyame. Way this sand's driftin', a man could easy make a mistake. I ain't gonna hold it against you."

Willoughby shook his head in disgust. "I'll

never understand why I listen to you and your wild ideas. It isn't enough you try to get me beaten to death, killed by a horse, or shot by bandits or an enraged father. Now you're going to let me die of thirst out here in the middle of nowhere."

"You still mad at me?"

Willoughby glared at Brubs. "If you hadn't brought that bottle from Symms's place I would have been halfway back to the Sabine River by now."

A quick grin flashed under Brubs's thick mustache, dusted white by alkali sand. "Takes a few jolts of red-eye to make a man see the true and proper path sometimes. Why, we weren't more'n halfway through that jug before you was ready to take on old Delgado all by your lonesome. You're just lucky I decided to come along in case you need some help."

"My luck," Willoughby muttered, "has taken a distinct turn for the worse since I met you." He sighed heavily. "From this point onward — if I live — I swear that liquor will never again touch my lips if one Brubs McCallan is within two hundred miles of where I happen to be."

Brubs licked his chapped lips. "Wish we'd brung a bottle of that LaQuesta rotgut along. Good, stiff drink sure would go down smooth right now." He chuckled softly. "Sounds like you're still a might peeved, partner. Maybe it ain't as bad as I made it sound. We ain't plumb lost. We know we're in Chihuahua, and that's

188

where Stump said Delgado hangs out."

"Chihuahua, in case you haven't noticed, is a big place." Willoughby lifted his canteen, shook it, and reluctantly dropped it back into place. "So what do we do now?"

Brubs pulled his hat down tighter against a gust of furnace-like wind. "Keep ridin' west. You quit frettin', Dave. Bad for your gut. We'll cut sign on a road pretty soon. There's Mexican villages all over the place." He waved a hand toward a line of mountains that shimmered blue and hazy on the far western horizon. "Even if they ain't no towns, them hills yonder ain't more than five, six days ride off, and where there's hills there's water. That black of yours is lookin' a tad gaunt in the flanks. He might be gettin' thirsty." He touched spurs to the sorrel.

Willoughby hesitated for a moment, resigned himself to perishing in the windswept desert, then clucked the black into motion.

The two rode in silence for several hours before Brubs checked his sorrel, turned in the saddle, and grinned at Willoughby. "What'd I tell you, partner?" He pointed ahead.

A narrow, dusty path marked by wheel tracks and hoofprints twisted its way between cactus clumps and Spanish dagger. Some of the tracks looked reasonably fresh.

"Cart road," Brubs said. "Where there's carts, there's people." He licked his lips. "Where there's people, there's a cool beer, and I done worked up a serious-type thirst. Get that fixed, then we'll find out where Delgado's at."

"How do we do that?"

"Easy, partner. We ask 'em."

Willoughby's brow furrowed. "What if they won't tell us? I remember you once said all Mexicans are cousins. Maybe they're Delgado's cousins."

Brubs waved a hand. "At least one of a Mex's cousins is always mad at him over somethin' and lookin' to get even. No need frettin' over it. You just leave it to your old Uncle Brubs."

Willoughby's tongue seemed to swell in his furred mouth as the black plodded along the dusty cart path beside Brubs's sorrel. Despite his earlier vow, Willoughby freely admitted to himself that he would probably kill for a cold beer at the moment. Another hour passed before a dun-colored cluster of adobe huts appeared through the shimmering heat waves.

The village was small, a jumble of shacks that reminded Willoughby of LaQuesta. Brubs waved to a stooped Mexican woman grubbing without enthusiasm in a wilted garden plot. She stared back in sullen curiosity, but didn't return the wave.

Willoughby had to pull on the reins to keep the thirsty black under control as they neared a wooden horse trough at the side of a building. The water looked stale and a bit scummy, but the black and Brubs's sorrel didn't seem to mind. They thrust noses in the water up past the nostrils and drank noisily. Brubs's nose wrinkled as he tested the breeze, then he nodded toward a small adobe and grinned at Willoughby. "Cantina. See, amigo? You ain't gonna die of thirst after all."

The cantina was dark and cool. As Willoughby's vision adjusted to the murkiness broken only by the light of a small window and a guttering oil lamp, he noticed that the place was also crowded. A half dozen tough-looking vaqueros leaned against the bar or sat at tables, beer mugs and whiskey glasses in hand or within easy reach. The expressions on their swarthy faces were not looks of welcome.

Willoughby ignored the sullen atmosphere and followed as Brubs strode to the bar. An elderly Mexican barely five feet tall and with stooped shoulders stood behind rough planks laid across empty beer kegs. Brubs held up two fingers. *"Dos cervezas, por favor,"* he said. He plucked a coin from his shirt pocket and dropped it on the splintery bar.

The Mexican glared at the two Anglos suspiciously, making no move to serve them.

Near Willoughby's side one vaquero, a broad-shouldered man with a narrow mustache, hard eyes, and a big pistol and even bigger knife belted at his waist, pointedly moved a couple of steps down the bar. The silence in the cantina was almost deafening, Willoughby thought. He felt a chill creep along his backbone.

The bartender finally stirred. He drew two beers from a wooden keg and placed them before the two men.

Brubs drained his mug without pausing for breath, wiped the foam from his mustache, and sighed in satisfaction. *"Muy bueno,"* he said heartily. He waved for refills before the aged Mexican had a chance to sit back down.

Willoughby forced himself to stop after a few swallows. Too much beer on a belly that had gone too many days with too little water had a tendency to hit bottom and come right back up. He put the mug down and glanced around. The chilly feeling worked its way further up his spine.

Every man in the place was armed and surly. Willoughby saw one figure at a corner table in the darkest part of the cantina who looked vaguely familiar, but the man had his sombrero pulled down over his eyes, the face in deep shadow.

Brubs downed half his second mug, then gestured to the bartender. *"¿Habla Inglés, amigo?"*

The bartender shook his head. There was no expression in the deep black eyes.

Brubs raised his voice. "Anybody here talk American?"

A stony silence was his only reply.

Brubs shrugged. "Well, partner," he said to Willoughby, "I reckon I'll just have to talk at 'em in their own lingo. First, we'll see where we can bed down for the night. Then I'll ask 'em about Delgado." He stepped around Willoughby to the big vaquero with the narrow mustache.

"Amigo," Brubs said to the big man, *"yo venir de —"* Brubs's voice faltered for an instant.

192

"*Cama suyo casa, esposa con*—" Willoughby saw the vaquero's eyes narrow. A flush seemed to spread in the dark cheeks. "*. . . pechos pequeño* — Oh, *Christ!*"

Brubs jumped backward, almost knocking Willoughby down. Willoughby staggered, regained his balance, and stood stunned, unable to move. The vaquero held the oversized knife in a ham-sized fist, the keen tip of the blade pointed at Brubs's gut. Brubs backpedaled, hands extended, palms outward. "Easy, amigo! What the hell?"

Willoughby heard the sudden clatter and scrape of chairs, the whisper of metal against leather. He tore his gaze from the knife and glanced around the room. Every Mexican there seemed to have a pistol in hand. And every one of them was pointed at the two Anglos. Willoughby braced himself to be blown away in a thunder of lead — the thought flitted through his mind that Brubs was already a dead man, sliced to bits for some unknown reason.

The big Mexican took a mincing step forward, his weight on the balls of his feet, knife poised for an upward slash that would gut Brubs like a butchered pig.

"*¡No pistolas! ¡Pedro, tranquilo!*"

The big man froze at the sharp bark from the shadows. Willoughby shot a quick glance toward the voice. The man at the darkened table rose to his feet, his right hand on the butt of the pistol at his hip. No one in the crowd moved for several heartbeats. It seemed to Willoughby that time had stopped. Then, one by one, the vaqueros holstered their weapons. The big man still held the knife as the man from the shadows strode soundlessly toward the confrontation. His features took shape in the dim light as he stopped beside Brubs and the big vaquero.

"Ignacio! God, am I glad to see you!" Brubs blurted. "What the hell's got into this crazy Mexican?"

A slight smile touched Ignacio Cruz's lips. Amusement twinkled in the wiry gunfighter's dark eyes. "I am not sure amigo, but I think he is angry with you."

"Good Christ, I got that part of it already," Brubs said. "What the hell did I do?"

Ignacio shrugged. "Perhaps a misunderstanding. If that is so, perhaps I can help. If not, Pedro will open your belly even if I shoot him first, and I would regret that, for he is my sister's husband." He turned and jabbered a quick spurt of Spanish to the big vaquero, listened to the mumbled reply, and turned back to Brubs. "Pedro says he will put the knife away if you apologize. I would recommend you make the apology a sincere one."

"Apologize? Damn right, I'll apologize. What for?"

"A moment ago, you told this man — in some of the worst Spanish I've ever heard — that you had just come from the bed in his home. And that his wife had small, saggy breasts."

194

"Oh, Jesus," Brubs moaned. "Is that what I said?"

"It is a reasonably close translation."

"No wonder he's got his back up. Ignacio, that wasn't what I meant." Brubs's tone was pleading. "Tell the big son of a — tell Señor Pedro I sure didn't mean no insult."

Ignacio rattled another Spanish phrase at the scowling vaquero. The big man's eyes still glittered in rage.

Brubs swallowed hard. "All I was tryin' to do was ask if there was a place where me and Dave could bed down for the night, maybe get us a woman. Ignacio, my Mex ain't too good. I swear to God I never seen this man's wife before, and I sure as hell ain't never seen her tits."

Ignacio turned back to the big man and talked softly for a few seconds. The fury slowly drained from the vaquero's flushed face. Finally, he shrugged, mumbled something, sheathed the knife, and turned away.

"Pedro accepts your profuse and sincere apology," Ignacio said to Brubs. "I took the liberty of embellishing your words a bit. I also told him you two were my friends. He will not kill you now."

Willoughby sagged against the bar, his knees weak.

Brubs's shoulders slumped in relief. "Ignacio, I owe you. I ain't been that close to the business end of a butcher knife but once, and I still get the 'fraids somethin' fierce when I think back

195

on it. I need a drink. Buy you one? And Pedro there, too?"

Ignacio Cruz's brow wrinkled. "I will join you, but perhaps it would be best if you did not speak again to Pedro. He is a dangerous man and has a quick temper."

"Couldn't help but notice. Maybe you better order for us, Ignacio. I might get somethin' wrong again." Brubs turned to Willoughby. "Want a drink, partner?"

Willoughby finally trusted his voice enough to speak. "Brubs McCallan," he said shakily, "you told me you could speak Spanish."

Brubs grinned as if nothing had happened. "Don't go gettin' yourself all fretted up again, Dave. I told you I spoke a little Mex, and that ain't no lie. I can order a beer and ask where the whorehouse is at. What else does a man need in Mexico?"

Willoughby glared at Brubs, the cold knot of raw fear in his gut thawing under a wash of anger. "At least I'll grant you one thing, Brubs — you came up with a brand new way to nearly get me killed."

Brubs clapped a hand on Willoughby's shoulder. "Aw, forget it, partner. Nothin' happened. I didn't have to shoot that Pedro feller after all, thanks to Ignacio here."

Dave dropped his head into his hands and groaned aloud.

"Is he ill?"

"Nah, Ignacio. He gets a touch of the vapors

ever' once in a while. He ain't got used to our ways yet."

Willoughby slowly raised his head. "Brubs, one of these days I'm going to be forced to shoot you myself. In self-defense."

Brubs said, "Well, maybe that was a little closer'n I wanted to cut it, I reckon. No harm done." He chuckled aloud. "Downright funny when I think on it. Somethin' to tell your grandkids about, you ever have any."

"I am delighted that you are amused, Mr. McCallan. And yes, I will have a drink. A big one. And then I'm going to have Señor Cruz ask the bartender if I might borrow a beer bottle."

Brubs laughed aloud. "Old Dave'll be all right now, Ignacio. He done coughed up that hairball he's been chokin' on."

Ignacio jabbered in rapid-fire Spanish to the aging bartender. "I do not enjoy standing while drinking," Ignacio said. "Join me at my table. Julio will deliver a bottle of tequila to us, and you may inform me of what brings you to Tres Perros."

"Tres Perros?"

"Three Dogs." Ignacio led the way to the table in the darkened corner. "My village. I was born in a small *jacal* here. The hut is gone now, but one's home does not crumble along with the walls."

The bartender reached the table almost as soon as the men, a bottle in one hand and three glasses in the other. *"Gracias, Julio,"* Brubs said, handing the hunched man a coin.

"Brubs," Willoughby snapped, "don't try talking any more Spanish!"

Brubs grinned and winked at Julio. "Dave gets touchy when he has the vapors." He picked up the bottle, poured a generous dollop into a glass, and handed it to Willoughby.

Willoughby picked up the glass, swallowed a hefty slug of the pale gold liquor, and came up sputtering and gasping for breath. His eyes watered. "What is this?"

"Aw, come on, partner. You mean you never had tequila before?"

"No. It's — different." Willoughby felt a sudden blast of heat in his belly.

Brubs chuckled. "Now you're a step closer to bein' a real, genuine Texan, Dave. Hang with me, boy, and we'll make one out of you yet."

Willoughby felt the simmering anger fade. "I'll probably hang with you all right, Brubs. The two of us most likely will share a stout tree limb or a gallows somewhere." He picked up the glass again. The second swallow went down a lot smoother.

Ignacio listened in courteous silence as Brubs told of the attack at Mustang Mesa, the killing of Stump Hankins, and the theft of the horses. "And that's how come we're in Three Dogs, amigo," he concluded. "We aim to get them horses back. Know anybody who can point us to where Delgado's hangin' out?"

Ignacio tossed back a shot of tequila and sighed. "I am sad to hear Stump Hankins is dead," he said solemnly. "He was a friend once, perhaps even my savior. He gave me, a stranger and a Mexican, a fresh horse when the *federales* were closing in on me south of the Rio Grande."

Willoughby's cheeks were beginning to feel numb. He wiped a hand across his forehead. It came away damp. He reached for the bottle.

Ignacio leaned back in his chair and stared at the ceiling for a moment. "Tonight you will be my guests, my gringo friends," he said. "We will eat, drink, and talk of things. I regret that I have no women to share." He sighed. "Tres Perros has much to offer. Unfortunately, women are not among its advantages."

"De nada."

"Brubs —"

"I know. Quit talkin' Mexican."

"I am familiar with Delgado's stronghold," Ignacio said. "I will take you there. We begin in the morning after acquiring supplies. It is a long ride, perhaps two days."

"Thanks, amigo." Brubs's words slurred a bit. "I reckon we owe you a couple more. Maybe someday we can pay back the favors."

Ignacio half smiled. "Perhaps. One never knows where one's path might lead."

Brubs McCallan leaned back against his saddle and stared at the stars overhead. It was kind of odd, he thought, that the stars didn't change that much. Texans and Mexicans had the same sky.

Brubs's tongue still felt a bit haired over from the tequila bout, but his headache was gone. That Mexican stuff packed a powerful kick the morning after, and it still stung some even after a full day's ride.

Dave Willoughby didn't seem to have the least bit of a hangover, which surprised Brubs a bit. Maybe Yankees were immune to tequila bites. Brubs made a mental note to test that idea again one of these days. It sort of smarted when a greenhorn Yankee army officer college boy drank a real purebred Texan under the table.

Willoughby hadn't even been cranky this morning. He'd stretched, shaved again — a waste of time, water, and perfectly good whiskers — and was downright chipper when he dragged Brubs out of the bedroll an hour before sunup. Willoughby even cooked breakfast and ate like a field hand. Brubs skipped the morning meal. He hadn't quite felt up to facing a fried egg. It looked like a big yellow eye staring back at him.

Willoughby didn't even grouse much about the little speck of trouble back in the Tres Perros cantina. He just sort of put a hard eye on Brubs and said, "If we're going to be in Mexico, I'd better learn the language myself. The current spokesman for this partnership knows enough ways to get us killed in English, let alone misapplied Spanish."

Willoughby and Ignacio had ridden stirrup to stirrup all day, ignoring Brubs's impending death from the fangs of the tequila tarantula. Willoughby asked the Spanish words for objects and phrases and repeated them back until he had them right. Ignacio seemed impressed at how fast Willoughby picked up on Mex, but Brubs figured anybody who savvied that Latin lingo ought to be able to handle Mexican pretty good. Brubs, for his part, had suffered in pained silence throughout the day.

Even now, Willoughby and Ignacio had their heads together at the camp fire, jabbering in Spanish and tying up a couple of new hackamores out of twisted horsehair. Willoughby might be quicker than a scalded cat at learning Mex, Brubs thought, but he couldn't hold a candle to Brubs McCallan when it came to tying the complex knots that went into a hackamore. They didn't teach that in no college.

He didn't hold it against Willoughby. Every man had his own talents, Stump Hankins had said once. It did sting a little bit when Stump added cranky-like that he hadn't figured out yet what Brubs McCallan was good at. Brubs missed the old badger. They didn't make men like Stump anymore.

The country had changed as they rode. The desert faded by slow miles into the distance. Grass began to appear more frequently, the spotty clumps crisp and brownish from lack of moisture. Now they were only a couple of days ride from the foothills of some high, jagged mountains Ignacio called the Sierra Madre. Ignacio Cruz knew every puddle of water, spot of grass, edible plant, and decent campsite in the whole country, it seemed. Made traveling a whole lot easier. And for a shooter, Ignacio wasn't a bad feller. Downright likeable, once you got to know him. Brubs made himself a promise never to cross Ignacio Cruz, though. Making that bowlegged little Mex mad could get a man dead in a hurry.

The soft mutter of Spanish and American words and the sound of horses cropping tall grass by the stream at the edge of the campsite was soothing to his ears. He felt his eyelids getting heavy, even though it was still on the young side of sack time. By sundown tomorrow, they'd know where Delgado was.

Brubs drifted off to sleep, contented.

Ignacio Cruz lay on his belly atop a rocky ridge and nodded toward the clump of buildings in the valley below. "Delgado's stronghold," he said softly to the men lying beside him.

Brubs McCallan studied the layout with care, committing it to memory before the lowering sun cloaked the stronghold in a blanket of shadow.

A sprawling adobe ranch house stood at the south end of a large rock corral which held several horses. A dozen saddles were propped along one wall of the corral. Brubs recognized a few of the horses from this distance, a quarter of a mile away. Stump Hankins's big roan, Choctaw, and the little mustang Brubs called Mouse stood head-to-tail in the middle of the corral. The coyote dun had his nose stuck into a pile of fodder. Stump's mules lazed hipshot, ears flopped, at the east fence. The brown lead mare rubbed her head against the one-eared mule's shoulder by the water trough. A quick study told Brubs that most of the band they had caught at Mustang Mesa were in the corral. Other horses were scattered, grazing, in the valley which led northeast toward the spot where the Conchos and Rio Grande joined.

Brubs turned his attention back to the stronghold itself. A jumble of rocks and cactus at the base of the west ridge formed a broken wall almost to the edge of the corral. A mesquite thicket began where the rockfall stopped and continued past the house. Getting to the place would be no problem. Getting out might be.

Four Mexicans sat outside the corral. It was hard to tell from here, Brubs conceded, but he was reasonably sure they were playing a card game of some sort. One mounted man prowled the grassy valley, keeping an eye on the horse herd. Brubs figured there were several others inside the house. Smoke drifted from a chimney; it was supper time.

"The place looks like a fortress," Dave Willoughby said softly. "Firing ports cut into the walls of the house. Nothing short of a six-pound cannon could break through those thick walls."

Ignacio nodded. "Delgado feels safe here. He is much less wary when in his stronghold. He keeps only one man standing watch at night." He pointed toward a wooden shack at a corner of the corral. The shack had two doors, one opening into the corral and a second leading to the yard of the big ranch house. "The sentry spends most of his watch in the shack. The man on watch often passes much of his time dozing, if he thinks Delgado will not catch him sleeping. The others bed down in the big house."

Brubs cast a quick glance at Cruz. "You sure know a lot about Delgado's habits, Ignacio." It was a question as much as a comment.

Ignacio shrugged. "I have often taken refuge here to escape the *federales*. Even government soldiers dare not venture into Delgado's lair. Delgado twice has asked me to ride with them, but I do not like some of his men. They are violent by nature." Ignacio turned to Brubs. "Do you plan to kill Delgado?"

"If I had my druthers," Brubs said calmly, "I'd just as soon didn't nobody get killed. I ain't happy with Delgado for killin' Stump, but that was a personal spat. All Dave and me want is to get our horses back."

Ignacio nodded. "That is good to hear. Delgado is not, at heart, a bad man, as are some of his associates. Delgado himself is merely an honest horse thief trying to make a few pesos." He glanced at the sun sliding behind the mountains. "Perhaps we should move back now, before someone in the stronghold happens to look up this way."

The three men crabbed back below the lip of the ridge, then strode toward their horses hidden below in a stand of junipers.

"Ignacio," Brubs said as they walked, "we could sure use some help. Why don't you join up with us? We'll cut you in for a share of the mustangs."

Ignacio shook his head. "I think not. I will sketch in the dirt a map of the quickest route to the Rio Grande, if you manage to get your horses back, then ride for the home of my cousin a few miles south of here." He paused to sniff the air. "I do not wish to be caught out in the open on horseback when the storm comes."

Brubs glanced at the cloudless sky. "What storm? Looks to me like it ain't rained here in quite a spell."

Ignacio started walking again. "It will come. I smell it, feel it in my bones. It will be a big storm with hard rain, much lighting, perhaps some hail. The clouds will come by midnight. The storm will break at dawn tomorrow, perhaps at mid-morning, but no later than noon."

Brubs glanced at the sky again. Nothing had changed. Not a cloud in sight. But the wind had shifted. It blew from the east now instead of the southwest. The breeze still smelled like desert to Brubs, but he wasn't going to argue with Ignacio. This was his country.

Sunset came quickly to the foothills of the Sierra Madre. Brubs stood at Ignacio Cruz's side in the fading light as the wiry gunfighter tightened the girth of his saddle. Ignacio offered a hand to Willoughby, then to Brubs. "Good fortune, my gringo friends," Ignacio said. "Perhaps we meet again."

"Ignacio, we're beholden to you," Brubs said solemnly. "Are you plumb sure you won't come with us?"

Ignacio's smile flashed in the near darkness. "No. I do not wish to take part in your quarrel with Delgado. We have blood ties, he and I."

"Let me guess," Brubs said. "Cousins?"

"By marriage." Ignacio mounted and raised his fingertips to the broad brim of his sombrero. *"Vaya con Dios, amigos,"* he said. He reined his horse about.

Brubs and Willoughby stood and watched as Ignacio rode from view. "Well, partner," Brubs finally said with a sigh, "I reckon it's time we start gettin' ready to go to work."

Willoughby cut a quick glance at Brubs. "I guess you're going to tell me this is just going to be a simple horseback ride? Nothing to it, correct?"

"That's right, partner."

"So all we have to do," Willoughby said wryly, "is ride down there and take a herd of horses from beneath the noses of a dozen or so tough men with big guns and bad tempers." He lifted an eyebrow. "I suppose you have a plan of action all worked out?"

Brubs grinned. "Sure 'nuff. Nothin' to it, partner. It'll go smooth as a baby's butt."

Willoughby groaned aloud. "Now I *know* it's time to worry."

TEN

Brubs McCallan crept silently through the mesquite thicket on hands and knees, his senses turned to every noise and rustle in the brush. The sky told Brubs it was just past three in the morning. The clouds were rolling in, as Ignacio had predicted.

So far, so good, Brubs thought. A few more yards and he'd be all set. The doors of the wooden shack at the corner of the corral stood open to the cool night air. A lantern inside turned the doorways into rectangles of golden yellow shadowed only by the movements of the sentry who had just gone on duty inside.

Brubs had removed his spurs and left his rifle behind with Willoughby and the saddled horses. If something went wrong and there was shooting, it would be handgun work down here, not a rifle job.

Willoughby waited a hundred yards away atop the ridge, ready to provide covering fire if necessary. Dave had fretted some about Brubs's going alone into the enemy camp, but finally shushed up when Brubs pointed out that this was a job for someone sneaky. And that meant infantry, not artillery.

Brubs paused to listen, trusting his ears more

than his eyes. He heard the rustle of clothing, a few footsteps, and then a splashing stream of fluid as the sentry stepped outside the shack and relieved himself. In a few minutes, with any luck at all, the sentinel would be dozing inside the wooden structure. Brubs clutched a wrist-sized chunk of mesquite limb loosely in his right hand. He would have preferred hickory for bashing heads, but the mesquite would do.

The night had cooled rapidly in the thin pre-dawn hours. The breeze blew from the west now, an occasional gust carrying the clean scent of rain. Brubs glanced at the sky above the western ridge. The stars were gone, blotted out by gathering thunderclouds. Lightning flickered almost constantly through the blackness of the cloud mountain. The rumble of distant thunder was faint to the ears. Brubs hoped the storm didn't break too soon. If it did, and the Rio Grande flooded, he and Willoughby would be trapped between the rolling waters and a sizeable band of angry men with guns. That idea hadn't set too well with Dave. He didn't share Brubs's notion that everything was going to work out all right. That was like Dave, Brubs mused. Always looking on the gloomy side.

Brubs settled in to wait. The storm clouds moved closer, the deep, guttural thunder becoming more distinct to the ear. A few of the horses stirred and snorted, restless, sensing the storm. Brubs glanced at the moon. He should have enough light to work by before the clouds covered the pale white sliver.

After a half hour the faint, buzzing sound of snoring reached Brubs's ears. He grinned to himself, gripped the mesquite club, and crept to the edge of the thicket. He could almost reach out and touch the wall of the shack now. He eased his way to the opening of the shelter and peeked inside.

The guttering lantern showed the Mexican sentry sitting against the wall, sombrero at his side, head tilted back, his mouth open. Brubs stepped inside the lean-to and swung the mesquite club.

The crack of wood against skull seemed awfully loud to Brubs, but the Mexican wouldn't be making any noise for a spell. He was out cold.

Brubs folded his hat, crammed it under his belt, picked up the Mexican's sombrero, and clapped it onto his own head. The fit was tight, but if anybody looked out and saw the big hat they'd probably figure it was just the sentry checking on things.

Brubs slipped his skinning knife from the sheath at his belt and stepped from the shack into the corral. He worked his way down the line of saddles propped against the fence, slicing through girth straps and stirrup leathers. He saved the last saddle, picked up a hackamore, and worked his way along the fence toward the grulla mustang. Mouse snorted and rolled his eyes, but stood his ground. Brubs would rather have caught Choctaw, but the big roan was on the far side of the corral. Brubs wasn't eager to cross that much open space just yet. Mouse would have to do.

"Easy, Mouse," Brubs said softly as he eased closer to the mustang. "You owe me, you sorry excuse of a flea-bit plug, and it's time to pay me back." The mustang nuzzled Brubs's ribs as he slipped the hackamore into place. He led the grulla to the saddle he had picked out and eased it onto Mouse. The grulla humped his back. "Damn you, Mouse, don't you go pitchin' on me now. You decide to buck me off, wait and do it in Texas."

He looped the hackamore reins through an iron ring set into the side of the wooden shed and glanced inside. The sentry he had clobbered was still unconscious. Brubs crept along the stone fence to the corral gate, staying in the inky shadows as long as possible. Then he took a deep breath, stepped into the open, slid back the bar latch of the gate, and gave it a shove. The creak of a hinge sounded like the scream of a panther as the gate swung back, but Brubs figured everything was all right so far because nobody had shot him yet. The thunder was closer now, the lightning flashes popping quick bursts of white light that illuminated the deepest shadows and played hob with a man's night vision. Brubs knew there was no more time to waste.

He made his way back to Mouse, stroked the

mustang's neck once, toed the stirrup, and swung aboard. Mouse laid his ears back along his neck, but the hump in his back flattened out. Brubs sighed in relief. The little grulla wasn't going to pitch — maybe. The stirrups on the stolen saddle were a couple of inches too long for Brubs's stubby legs, but he figured this wasn't a time to get overly persnickety. He reined Mouse along the back fence, silently waving his free hand at the horses. They stirred, then began to edge toward the gate.

The brown mare was the first to sense freedom. She trotted through the opening, the one-eared mule at her hip. Choctaw trotted over and fell into step behind the mule. Other horses followed her lead; Brubs made a quick estimate during a lightning flash and figured he had nearly twenty head moving from the corral into the open valley. The moon vanished behind a wall of clouds. Another lightning flash illuminated the valley, burning the image of scattered pairs and small groups of horses into Brubs's brain. He glanced over his shoulder, his heartbeat quickening. "Mouse," he whispered, "this is going too damned easy —"

A hoarse yell sounded from the back of the corral. Brubs glanced over his shoulder, saw the red blossom of a muzzle blast, and instinctively ducked. He heard the slug from the pistol shot hum past his ear. He slammed his heels into Mouse's ribs. "Hardest-headed Mex I ever seen," Brubs muttered. Another slug buzzed past, too close for comfort. "Bastard can shoot, too." Brubs whipped the big sombrero from his head and waved it, whooping and yelling. The horses, spooked by the combination of lightning, gunshots, and sudden yells, broke into a run. A jagged tongue of lightning streaked overhead as a bone-jarring thunderclap hammered at Brubs's ears. The light from the bolt seemed to linger. Horses from across the meadow raced to join the fleeing band. Another pistol slug fell behind Mouse, splatting harmlessly into the valley turf. Brubs knew he was out of pistol range. He leaned over the grulla's neck. "Mouse, I hope you can run in the dark," he said.

A rifle shot cracked, then another. Brubs glanced up at the ridge and saw two more quick muzzle flashes, heard the startled yells from behind, and figured Willoughby's rifle had driven any shooters to cover. Then Mouse, close behind the horse herd, pounded past the ridge and out of gun range from the corral.

The horses thundered up the valley, racing toward the northeast. Brubs breathed a quick grunt of relief. The horses were headed in the right direction. He wouldn't have to worry about turning them until he'd put some air between himself and Delgado's bunch.

The horses ran hard for two miles, then finally began to slow, winded in the quick, hard sprint. Brubs checked the grulla back to a long lope. Mouse was blowing a bit, but there was no sign of fatigue in the tight-twisted little mustang's muscles. Lightning flashed almost constantly now, the thunderclaps packed one atop the other. A fat raindrop slapped against Brubs's shoulder. The tension abruptly flowed from his muscles. "By God, Mouse, we done it!" Brubs yelled in exuberance. "We're goin' back to Tex—"

The shout ended in a choked yelp as Mouse went down and Brubs's face slammed into the dirt. He felt the quick, heavy slam of the horse's rump against his back as the mustang rolled over him. Lights flashed in Brubs's head and went out.

Brubs struggled back to consciousness, aware that something was shaking his shoulders. He spat out a mouthful of grass and dirt.

"Brubs! You hurt?" The near-constant lightning illuminated Dave Willoughby's face as he knelt over Brubs, the reins of the saddled black and sorrel in hand.

"Back —" Brubs croaked. His shirt was stuck to his back. "Horse fell. Blood?"

"Rain."

Brubs became aware of the hammering of raindrops against his back and legs and felt a surge of relief. If he could feel the rain, at least his back wasn't broken. "Horses?"

"Up ahead. I was a couple hundred yards behind you when I saw your horse go down during a lightning flash." Willoughby almost had to yell to be heard above the thunder and increasing drum of pounding rain. "Can you move?"

"Don't want to."

Brubs felt Willoughby's hand slip beneath his arm. "We've got to get out of here, Brubs!"

"Mouse?"

"Oh, for Christ's sake, the damned horse is all right! I saw him get up and run toward the herd!" Willoughby heaved Brubs to his feet and almost threw him into the saddle aboard the sorrel. "We have to ride! Delgado'll be after us any minute!"

"Won't," Brubs grunted. He knew he was still about half-stunned because he hadn't started hurting yet. "I cut up their saddles — run off their horses."

"Tell it to those four men back there coming at us!" Willoughby yanked his rifle from the saddle scabbard. "Ride, Brubs! I'll cover you!"

The news jolted Brubs closer to reality. His head spun. He barely had the strength to rein the sorrel around and nudge the rangy gelding into a run. He heard two rifle shots, then another, close behind. He chanced a glance over his shoulder. A lightning flash revealed Willoughby kneeling in the mud, firing toward dark shapes in the near distance. Another flash a split second later showed one of the shapes going down.

The sheets of pounding rain finally brought Brubs back among the living and fed new strength into his bruised muscles. He reined the sorrel around, pulled his handgun, and spurred back toward the stronghold. He almost shot Willoughby by mistake as the black raced toward him, mud flying from churning hooves.

"Wrong way, dammit!" Willoughby shouted as he sped by.

Brubs fired a couple of wild shots, partly to send a message to the bandit riders and partly just for the hell of it, then reined his horse about and raced after Willoughby. The sorrel caught up with Dave's black within a half mile. The horse herd moved at a winded but steady trot a hundred yards ahead.

"You hit one of 'em!" Brubs yelled to Willoughby as he pulled alongside.

"If I did, it was dumb luck," Willoughby shouted back over the tumult of the storm. "I was just making noise."

"Whatever, it worked! Them jaspers lost interest in gettin' any closer to us right quick!"

"Quit yammering and ride, Brubs!" Willoughby yelled. "We've got another ten miles yet to Texas!"

The rain had slowed to a drizzle by the time the black of night gave way to a dull gray dawn. The storm was miles away now, the thunder faint in the distance. Brubs had regained full use of his senses. His back ached, but he knew it was just a bruise. It had been a near thing, though. If the horn or cantle of the saddle had hit him instead of Mouse's rump, it would have broken his back or squashed some ribs for sure. He was glad Mouse wasn't thirteen hundred pounds of draft horse.

Brubs realized he had lost the Mexican's sombrero in the fall. He pulled his crumpled and now muddy hat from beneath his belt and jammed it onto his head.

Several of the horses that had been lagging behind suddenly wheeled away from the cavvy and trotted back toward the stronghold. Willoughby started to turn his black to head them off.

"Let 'em go, partner!" Brubs yelled. "We still got plenty! We got to get across the Rio before the water gets too high or them gents back there stir up enough guts to try and catch up with us!"

Brubs heard the low, menacing rush of water well before they topped the rise on the south bank of the Rio Grande crossing. The ford was right where Ignacio Cruz said it would be. The brown lead mare seemed to have read Ignacio's map in the dirt. She had headed straight for the crossing. Brubs felt a quick rush of relief as he glanced at the river. It was only half full, not deep enough to swim a horse yet. He reached out and clapped Willoughby on the shoulder.

"We got it made now, partner," Brubs said. "All we got to do is get 'em across in the next five minutes, before the high water gets here."

Willoughby stared wide-eyed at the muddy red water for a couple of heartbeats. "It looks high enough right now."

"Give a listen. You hear that rumble?"

Willoughby nodded.

"That's the big water. Pretty soon a whole wall of it'll come through here. It'll be twenty feet deep in a few minutes." Brubs watched the brown mare trot down to the water's edge, snort, and paw at the muddy bank. "That mare's not real keen on bustin' into the Rio," Brubs said. "You take the point. She'll follow your black across."

"Brubs, I can't —"

"Don't fuss at me now, Dave Willoughby!" Brubs snapped. "We ain't got time to argue. Just get that black in the water."

"I can't —"

"Git, dammit! I'll push the drags." He shucked his rifle from the scabbard. "If you're spooked of a little water, this way you'll be the first across. I'll handle them bandits follerin' us if they get any closer."

Willoughby still hesitated. His face was ash-white in the gray light from the overcast sky. Brubs whacked Willoughby's black on the butt with the stock of his rifle. The black jumped, startled, and bolted, slipping and sliding down the slope of the ford toward the river. The horse hesitated only a split second at water's edge, then bunched its muscles and leapt into the stream. The brown mare followed almost immediately.

Brubs rode back and forth behind the trailing horses, whooping and yelling to urge them along. The rumble of flood waters drew closer.

Brubs worked frantically until the last horse was in the river, struggling against the swift current, then slapped heels to his sorrel.

The sorrel was an experienced river horse. Brubs gave him his head and looked up as Willoughby's black scrambled up the far bank, then stopped and shook itself like a big dog. Brubs grinned despite himself. He knew what an aggravation it was to have a horse do that under a man. Willoughby was back in Texas now, along with most of the horses.

The rumble from upriver grew to a thunderous roar. Brubs glanced upstream and felt the quick push of urgency in his gut. Still, he didn't rush the sorrel. A good river horse knew that sound as well as any man did. He felt the gelding nervously quicken its pace, splashing water as it plowed through the rising river.

The sorrel hit the far bank, almost went down as a front foot slipped in the mud churned and slicked by the horse herd, then regained its footing and lunged up the bank. Brubs glanced over his shoulder. A huge swell of muddy water a full six feet high surged down the river, whole trees tumbling at the crest of the sudden rise. The raging water crashed past only a few feet behind Brubs's winded sorrel.

Brubs pulled the horse to a stop on high ground and looked back. The Rio Grande was two hundred yards wide and fifteen feet deep already, and still rising. Three horsemen came into view atop the slope of the south bank. They stopped their horses and sat the saddles, staring at the muddy river. One of the riders seemed vaguely familiar.

"Too late, boys," Brubs said with a chuckle. He dismounted, knelt in the mud, and shouldered his rifle. He knew full well the three horsemen were out of effective range of the puny .44 rimfire, but he elevated the muzzle and squeezed off a couple of shots anyway. Both slugs fell well short of the horsemen, but they wheeled their mounts and spurred out of sight over the rise.

Brubs remounted, made a quick check of the cavvy, stripped the stolen saddle and hackamore from Mouse, and tossed them aside. None of the horses were hurt. A wide grin creased his mud-spattered face as he rode back to Willoughby. "By damn, partner, we done it!" Brubs whooped. "Got most all our horses back from that thief Delgado and better'n twenty of his own mounts to boot. We're gonna be rich men —" He paused abruptly, staring at Willoughby. "What the hell's the matter with you?"

Willoughby shivered violently, his right hand locked in a death grip on the saddle horn. His face was the color of flour gravy, his eyes glazed as he stared toward the roiling red waters of the river below.

"You hurt, Dave?"

Willoughby never took his eyes from the river. "No, I'm not hurt. It's just that — I've never been quite that scared before."

Brubs snorted. "Boogered at a little trickle of water like that?"

"If that's a trickle," Willoughby said through chattering teeth, "I hope to Christ I never see a flood."

"Hell, we made it across without no trouble and didn't lose a single horse. Ain't nothin' to worry about."

"Yes, there is," Willoughby said, his voice quavering. "I can't swim."

Brubs lifted an eyebrow. "Didn't know that, amigo. Reckon that old Rio in flood might be a bit spooky to a man can't swim. You ever cross a high-water river horseback before?"

Willoughby shook his head.

Brubs shrugged. "You'll get used to it. First time's the worst time. We'll be crossin' a lot more rivers before we're done."

Willoughby slowly lifted his gaze from the raging water to stare at Brubs. "I don't know where you keep coming up with this *we* crap, Brubs McCallan. Now you've added drowning to your impressive arsenal of plans for my death."

Brubs's lower lip protruded in a mock pout. "You sure don't show much gratitude for all the learnin' I've give you son. Come on — we'll move these horses up a few miles, set up camp, get you dried out and some hot grub in your belly. You'll feel good as new when we point this cavvy toward Goliad."

"Brubs?"

"What now?"

"I lost the possibles sack crossing the river. I guess it came untied and slipped off my saddle."

Brubs's brow wrinkled for an instant, then gave way to a reassuring grin. "That don't matter one whit. Wasn't no whiskey in it, nohow."

"Brubs, you don't understand. We don't have a single damn thing to eat."

Brubs clapped Willoughby on the shoulder. "That don't matter none, neither. Now, I ain't sayin' I might not be a touch cranky without my mornin' coffee, but a real genuine Texan can eat right good off the land."

Willoughby's eyes narrowed. "Is there anything a real genuine Texan can't do?"

Brubs chuckled. "Not that I know of. Speakin' of which, you done showed another sign of gettin' Texanized. Today's the first day I ever heard you cuss. Done pretty fair at it, too, even if they was just little lace drawers cusswords." He reined his horse around. "Come on, amigo. We got some horses to tend."

Brubs McCallan lay flat on his back beside a mesquite, unable to breathe, the breath knocked from his lungs. The coyote dun stood a few feet away. Brubs thought the horse looked mighty damn smug.

Dave Willoughby trotted up on Choctaw, eased the rangy roan to a stop, and sat in the saddle, forearms crossed over the horn. A slight smile touched his lips as he looked down at his partner. "Think it's time you gave up?"

Brubs finally managed to pull a breath of air into his chest. "No, by God," he gasped. "I'll get that . . . damn fool horse rode . . . yet."

"I don't know about that," Willoughby said casually. "That's the third time he's bucked you off today, and I would have to say he looks a lot fresher than you do."

Brubs sat up, decided nothing was broken, and glared at the coyote dun. The horse's ears were perked toward Brubs as if asking whether the man on the ground was hurt. Brubs brushed dirt and mesquite leaves from his pants. He was beginning to get a touch out of sorts with the coyote dun. "Don't you give me that smart-ass look," Brubs told the horse. "You ain't whupped me yet."

Willoughby chuckled softly. "I'll put a dollar on the dun."

Brubs glared at Willoughby. "Didn't know you was that much of a gamblin' man."

"It doesn't seem to be that much of a gamble," Willoughby said, a twinkle in his eyes. "I'm beginning to wonder if you're losing your touch with the rough string, partner."

Brubs heaved himself to his feet. "There ain't no need to go and hurt my feelin's like that, Dave Willoughby." He was starting to get a little peeved. "You know damn well that's the rankest buckin' horse a man ever forked." He glared at the coyote dun. "Saddle-broke, Stump says. Tryin' to get me killed from the grave, that old badger." He turned back to Dave. "I'll just by

God cover that dollar bet of yours — but we're gonna change the rules."

"What do you have in mind?"

"Get your saddle off that roan," Brubs said. "I'm tired of your raggin' me, and it's time you got a mouthful of dirt for once. We're tradin' horses. *You* got to ride the damn dun, and I'm bettin' *my* dollar on the horse."

The grin faded quickly from Willoughby's face. He raised a hand. "Now, wait a minute —"

"Get that saddle off," Brubs snapped. "It's high time you put up or shut up, Willoughby." He strode to the dun and started loosening the cinches.

Willoughby's knuckles whitened as he gripped the horn of his saddle. "I'm no bronc rider —"

Brubs cast a heated glare at Willoughby. "You gonna get down, or do I have to yank you off that roan and whup you?" He dropped his saddle and stared at Willoughby, hands on his hips.

"Brubs, you can't be serious."

"Never been seriouser. By God, it's my turn to giggle when you get your butt ironed out by some walleyed bronc."

Willoughby hesitated, his gaze flitting from the coyote dun to Brubs and back to the horse. Then he cautiously stepped down and stripped his saddle from the roan.

"I'm gonna enjoy this," Brubs said as he watched the pale-faced Willoughby saddle the dun.

Willoughby squared his shoulders and toed the stirrup.

Brubs's jaw dropped.

The coyote dun didn't hump up. He didn't even back his ears or snort. He moved out in a smooth, easy fox-trot, head carried low, ears perked forward. Willoughby put the dun into a slow lope, then reined the horse in a figure eight. The dun switched leads like a highly trained cutting horse. Willoughby pulled him to a sliding stop, then touched the reins first to the left side, then the right, of the dun's neck. The horse ducked its rump and spun, catlike, in the direction Willoughby asked.

He rode the coyote dun for a good fifteen minutes, putting the gelding through intricate maneuvers, then trotted back to Brubs's side. Willoughby sat easy, relaxed in the saddle.

"Just like a rocking chair," Willoughby said. "Soft mouth, quick and light on his feet, but smooth." He leaned forward and patted the dun's neck. "This may be the best horse I ever sat on." He raised an eyebrow at Brubs. "Looks like you owe me a dollar."

Brubs stared at the coyote dun. "That damn horse is doin' his level best to make a fool out of me. I ain't payin' you no dollar until you ride that idiot through one of them pitchin' fits." He abruptly yanked his hat from his head and sailed it between the horse's front feet.

The dun never twitched.

After a few seconds Willoughby gently pulled

225

back on the reins. The dun backed up a couple of steps and stopped, Brubs's hat crushed beneath a front hoof, eyes alert and ears perked forward.

"I don't think he's going to pitch with me, Brubs." There was a note of triumph in Willoughby's tone. "I'm going to enjoy spending that dollar."

Brubs snorted. "Don't go gettin' too smug. It's still a day's ride from here to LaQuesta. I'm doublin' the bet. Two bucks says that somewhere betwixt here and there, that horse is gonna poot your butt twelve feet in the air."

"I'll cover the bet," Willoughby said calmly. "Are you going to stand there all day pouted up like a setting hen, or are you going to saddle up and help me trail some horses? I'm getting a little tired of living off the land. In fact, I'm developing an outright aversion to jackrabbit meat."

"If you'll get that idiot horse off my hat, we'll go." The frown faded from Brubs's face. "I reckon it'll be nice to get back to LaQuesta, lay over a day to rest the horses, and have us a little fun." He retrieved his hat, punched it back into a semblance of its original battered state, and jammed it back onto his head. "I been gettin' a hankerin' for a touch of bad whiskey and more than a tad curious about that whore Symms mentioned." He swung the saddle into place and cinched up. "How much cash money we got left?"

"Twenty-five or so. Enough to buy supplies." Willoughby scowled as Brubs mounted. "I'm not going to let you spend it all on liquor and women, Brubs McCallan. You might as well get used to that idea right now. I am *not* eating rabbit all the way from LaQuesta to Goliad."

Brubs cast a wounded glance at his partner. "Dave Willoughby, you are the most suspicious, down-in-the-mouth feller I ever rode with, and that's a pure fact. Just about the time I get to thinkin' you might make a Texan after all, you go tryin' to spoil a man's hard-earned fun. Did I say somethin' about spendin' all our cash on whiskey and whores?"

"You didn't have to. I know how the wind blows where you ride."

Brubs waved a hand. "It don't matter none. Symms's whore's likely as ugly as he is. If that's a fact, she sure ain't gonna be worth no five dollars." He touched spurs to the roan. "Let's go, amigo. Quit dawdlin' — we got horses to move before that river goes down enough for old Delgado to come after us." He cocked an eyebrow at Willoughby. "Did one of them fellers back there look familiar to you?"

Willoughby's brow wrinkled. "Now that you mention it, one did — the way he sat his horse and all."

"Sure 'nuff did," Brubs said, his tone grim. "I'd near swear on a case of good whiskey that damn Brazos feller was one of 'em." The solemn expression abruptly faded, replaced by a spreading grin. "Let's get on to LaQuesta and see just how ugly old Symms's whore is, partner."

ELEVEN

"My, my," Brubs McCallan said, his words a bit slurred, "lookie what we got here."

Dave Willoughby lifted his gaze from the beer mug before him to the rickety stairs leading to the second floor of Symm's Dry Godds & Salon.

A bosomy blonde stood at the top of the stairs, an ample hip cocked to one side, her hand resting against the worn banister. The faded blue dress she wore strained at the seams, the three top buttons either missing or opened. She was staring at Willoughby, eyebrows raised.

Barley Symms, his eyes glazed from a quart of house whiskey, glanced at the woman and grunted. "Boys, this here is Katherine. Most everybody calls her Kat. She's the whore I was telling you about."

Willoughby courteously removed his hat, his face flushed in embarrassment, and nodded to the woman on the stairs. Brubs made no effort to uncover his head. "By damn, Symms," Brubs said, "she ain't half bad. I was expectin' some old smooth-mouthed Mex hag."

Kat strode quickly down the stairs. Her bouncy steps triggered impressive jiggles under the thin dress.

"Like a couple Jerseys at milkin' time," Brubs

muttered in awe. "Maybe a bit on the chunky side, but the chunks is sure enough in the right places."

Willoughby had to admit Brubs was right. Kat was a bit thick in the hips and waist and maybe a touch heavy of leg, but even at that her overall design still seemed to be somewhat top-heavy. She stepped to the bar alongside Willoughby.

"Hello, boys," she said. Her voice was husky, but somehow musical. "Welcome to LaQuesta."

"Kat, meet a couple new customers," Symms said. The saloon owner seemed to have trouble focusing his eyes. "The tall, clean one's Dave Willoughby. Little grubby one's Brubs McCallan." Symms pulled the cork from another jug, lifted it to his lips, and lowered the level in the bottle by a couple of inches.

"Pleased to meet you, fellas," Kat said, glancing from one to the other before her gaze settled on Willoughby. Kat's eyes were deep blue, almost indigo, and sprinkled with tiny gold flecks that sparkled in the light from the oil lamp. A faint line of freckles spread across the bridge of a long nose that had a bit of a rise in the middle. She had an honest sort of face, Willoughby thought, a childish trust in her blue eyes. She tossed her head, flipping shoulder-length blond hair that looked to be fresh from an extended brushing. It glistened in the lamplight. She might be a bit short of truly attractive, Willoughby thought, but looking at her didn't make a man's belly hurt. He dropped his gaze, unsure of what to say. It was difficult enough to talk to a respectable woman, let alone a prostitute.

Brubs McCallan labored under no such uncertainty.

"Say, Kat," he said, "how's about you and me goin' upstairs?"

Willoughby felt his face flush. "Brubs, don't you think you should at least offer to buy the lady a drink first?"

Brubs flashed a quick grin. "Dave, son, this ain't exactly like courtin'. It's business."

"Five dollars," Symms muttered. He swayed and almost fell from his stool behind the bar. He took another drink. "Each. In advance."

Brubs turned to the saloon owner. "Symms, you know we ain't got ten dollars left. This here saddle tramp I ride with done give most of it to you already. Wasted it on grub." He shook his head sadly. "Dave just ain't been able to get his necessaries straight ever since I whupped him in a saloon fight over to San 'Tone a spell back." He glanced at Willoughby. "How much we got left, partner?"

"Eight dollars and some change."

"Symms, how's about cuttin' a deal? Say, eight dollars and the three of us go upstairs together."

Symms squared his shoulders with an effort. "This here's a respectable place, McCallan. I ain't gonna have no pre— preversions in here. You go upstairs, you go one at a time." He reached for the bottle. It was already half-empty.

"Price is five dollars. You don't like it —"

"I know," Brubs interrupted, "it ain't but fifty miles to the next whore."

Willoughby knew Brubs was nearing three sheets to the wind, as the sailors said of their shore leave drinking bouts. He glanced at Kat, who had eased a bit closer to his side. He was uncomfortably conscious of the warmth from her body and tried his best to keep from looking down the front of her unbuttoned dress. "Miss, I apologize for my friend's behavior," Willoughby said. "He seems to be immune to the acquisition of gentlemanly manners, talking about you as if you were a side of beef or something."

Kat smiled, flashing even white teeth. The smile creased dimples into her cheeks. "Don't worry about it," she said softly. "I'm used to it."

Willoughby turned to Brubs. "There's no use haggling over the price. The issue is moot."

"Talk American. What you mean, smoot?"

"Moot. That means it's already settled. We are not going to spend any more money. We may need it before we reach Goliad."

Brubs grinned and clapped Willoughby on the shoulder. "Now, partner, what do we need money for? There ain't no place to spend money 'tween here and Goliad. Nothin' but rattlers and lizards, and they come free." He dropped his hand away. "Ain't that right, Symms?"

The saloon owner nodded. "Pure enough fact,

I reckon." Willoughby could barely make out Symms's mumbled words. The man was past three sheets in the wind; he was flying a full spread of canvas. Willoughby wondered how much longer Symms could ride that stool before it bucked him off.

"See, amigo?" Brubs said. "That's done settled. Now, you wouldn't turn down a man dyin' of thirst if he asked for a drink of water, would you?"

"That's different."

"Don't see how. I'm thirstin' awful bad, and Kat here's got the only canteen handy. Give Symms his five dollars so Kat and me can go upstairs."

"No."

Brubs's tone turned indignant. "After all I done for you, Dave Willoughby, that's a mighty poor thanks. Plumb ungrateful, that's what." He turned away, pouting, and sipped from his shot glass.

Willoughby sighed heavily, shrugged in resignation, and pulled a five-dollar gold piece from his pocket. "It just might be worth it not to have to listen to you whine and complain all the way to Goliad." He dropped the coin on the bar. Symms had to reach for it twice before his fingers touched the coin. It took him two more tries to pick it up.

"Now, that's my partner," Brubs said with a happy grin. He cuffed Willoughby on the shoulder. "Too bad you're gettin' short-sheeted this time, amigo, but I'll make it up to you. Old Brubs McCallan always pays his debts." Brubs reached for Kat's arm. "Come on, honey. I got this here awful bad itch."

Kat cast a quick glance over her shoulder at Dave as Brubs led her toward the stairs. Willoughby saw something flicker in her eyes, but couldn't read the message. Women always had been a mystery to him, a book written in a language he didn't speak and had never bothered to learn.

He downed the last of his beer as a door closed upstairs, and turned to Barley Symms. "Kat seems like a nice lady," he said. "How did she happen to wind up in LaQuesta?"

Symms downed another drink and leaned precariously on the bar stool. "Kat's my wife."

Willoughby sat stunned, not believing what he had just heard. "You mean to tell me you sell your own wife to total strangers?"

Symms swiped a bar rag across the sweat on his forehead. "Like money a damn sight more'n I like her," Symms said. "Fat sow don't do nothing but nag a man who drinks a little time to time. I ain't using her. Might as well make a dollar off those who do, 'cause she'd likely give it away free if I wasn't watching her."

"But, doesn't it bother you? I mean . . ." Willoughby's voice trailed off. He wasn't quite sure how to say exactly what he meant.

"Hell, no, it don't bother me," Symms muttered. "Any reason it should? Whore's a whore."

Willoughby finally shrugged. "I suppose it's none of my business." He was getting a bit uncomfortable with the conversation. "I would like another beer."

Symms grunted, rose from the bar stool, took one step toward the beer keg, and fell flat on his face. He didn't move. Willoughby stepped around the bar and knelt beside Symms. The man was breathing, puffing dust from the saloon floor, but he had passed out cold. Willoughby turned Symms's head so that he would be able to breathe better, then rose. He glanced around, picked up his mug, and drew himself a brew from the keg. He felt a touch of guilt over the idea of stealing from the helpless, so he dropped a dime on the bar and returned to his seat.

Brubs was back in fifteen minutes, a big grin spread across his ruddy face. He sagged against the bar and reached for a shot glass. "Man, that Kat's somethin'," he said. "Done took all the starch out of my knees. I ain't felt this good since that redhead up in Denton. Where's Symms?"

Willoughby gestured toward the floor behind the bar. "Passed out. It appears he has consumed too much of his own inventory."

Brubs chuckled, reached across the bar, and came up with a bottle. "Bald-headed old coot's been chargin' us three prices for ever'thing we bought here." He twisted the cork from the whiskey bottle. "Might as well make ourselves a discount." He hefted the bottle and swallowed twice. "By the by, amigo, Kat says if old Symms was passed out, you can come upstairs if you want. She figured Barley had about hit the end of his whiskey rope and tripped hisself."

"I don't have five dollars, Brubs."

Brubs grunted. "Kat said you could have it free."

"Why would she say that?"

Brubs's brow wrinkled in puzzlement. "Damned if I know, partner, but was I you, I sure wouldn't ask why. Go have a little fun. Get the kinks yanked out of your rope. Just don't be all night about it. We got to move them horses out come daylight." He swigged at the bottle.

Willoughby headed for the stairs.

Dave Willoughby rode the point, relaxed in the saddle, enjoying the effortless foxtrot of the coyote dun beneath him and the cool, misty fog that wisped along the faint trail. The fog brought a welcome break from the heat and dust of the last few days on the trail from LaQuesta.

In a couple of hours, if Brubs's navigation was accurate — not necessarily a given, Willoughby conceded from painful experience — they would reach the more distinct road to Goliad. Then it was only a half day's ride to Bass Jernigan's ranch west of Mission LaBahia, where hundreds of Texans had been executed by Mexican troops during the revolution. Willoughby wondered idly what the weather had been like some forty years ago, when the Texans were marched from the adobe fortress to their mass grave.

He twisted in the saddle to study the horses trailing behind. The brown mare was in the lead as usual, her belly distended by the foal she carried. She would be foaling in a couple of months. The one-eared mule trotted along at the mare's hip, Willoughby's black and Stump Hankins's roan close behind. Beyond the leaders, Willoughby could make out the increasingly vague shapes of about half the cavvy before the light fog and mist obscured the remainder of the herd strung out over almost a quarter of a mile.

Brubs rode drag, mounted on the little grulla mustang. Sounds carried well in the damp air. Willoughby heard Brubs's occasional good-natured curses aimed at horses dawdling in the rear of the cavvy, even though he couldn't see him.

The drive from LaQuesta had been surprisingly easy. The mix of captured mustangs and stolen Mexican horses had settled down and grown trail-wise between the distant Big Bend and the rolling, grassy, tree-studded country of south central Texas.

The mule suddenly stopped, nostrils flared, its remaining ear at attention, looking past Willoughby's shoulder. He turned in the saddle and abruptly checked the coyote dun. His heart leapt in his chest.

A big, bearded man sat astride a blaze-faced bay horse in the middle of the trail. He held a Springfield rifle in the crook of an arm, the muzzle trained on Willoughby's shirtfront. The bore of the rifle looked as big as a prairie dog hole.

"Howdy," the big man said. It wasn't a pleasant greeting.

"Good morning," Willoughby replied warily.

"Keep your hands away from that there pistol, son, and you won't get yourself dead. Now, what you doin' on my road?" Bushy eyebrows bunched over cold black eyes.

Willoughby pointedly kept his hands well away from the revolver at his waist. "Your road? I wasn't aware this was private property, sir." His fingers went cold on the reins.

"It is. This here's Jake Clanton's road. I'm him."

Willoughby tore his gaze from the black hole in the rifle muzzle and waited, not sure what was going on but feeling more uncomfortable by the second.

"It's a toll road." The man called Clanton squinted past Willoughby at the horse herd. "You got to pay to use it. Four bits a head's horse fare."

Willoughby heard the pad of horse's hooves on grass. Brubs pulled Mouse to a stop alongside Dave. "What's goin' on here?"

"This gentleman says he owns this road," Willoughby said cautiously, "and that we have to pay to use it."

Brubs snorted. "In a pig's butt. This here is public range. We ain't payin' one thin dime —"
The sound of a heavy hammer being drawn to

full cock cut short his objection.

"Then I reckon you boys'll just have to turn those horses over to me." Clanton's tone was cold. "Or maybe you both want to get yourselves killed."

Brubs's spine stiffened. He glared at the bearded man. "Look here, feller," he said through clenched teeth, "we worked too damn hard for them horses to just smooth hand 'em over to you. And in case you ain't looked, there's two of us and just one of you."

The expression on Clanton's face never changed. "Tell your partner that. I'll blow a hole bigger'n a pork chop through him if either of you so much as bats an eye. Now shuck them pistols, slow and easy. This old Springfield's got a hair trigger."

"Brubs, I think this man is serious," Willoughby said. He glanced at Brubs. The stocky Texan's jaw was set firm, eyes narrowed. It looked for all the world like Brubs was a heartbeat away from grabbing for his handgun.

For a long moment the tension was thick on the foggy road. Then Brubs shrugged. "Aw, what the hell, partner. I reckon it'd be better to pay the man than to have to kill him." He eased the Colt from his holster and let it drop. Willoughby followed suit. "Get the man his money, Dave," Brubs said.

"Brubs, we don't have any money." Willoughby heard the note of desperation in his own voice.

"Sure we do, partner," Brubs said with a knowing glance at Dave. "In that off side saddlebag of yours, where I put it after that little trouble over at Mustang Mesa. I'll fetch it." He started to dismount.

A chill worked up Willoughby's spine as he realized what Brubs was driving toward. The Colt taken from the dead Mexican bandit was still in his saddlebag.

"Hold it!"

Brubs paused, his right foot poised above the grulla mustang's rump. The rifle shifted toward Brubs.

"You there," Clanton barked at Willoughby, "you fetch the money. Somethin' tells me not to put a lot of faith in this ugly little friend of yours. Don't get stupid on me or there won't be nothin' left of him for the buzzards."

Willoughby slowly dismounted. He wiped the sweaty palm of his hand against his shirt, glanced at Brubs, and caught the almost indiscernible nod. He unbuckled the flap of the saddlebag and reached inside. His fingers closed over the walnut grips of the bandit's Colt.

"How long you been robbin' people thisaway, Clanton?" Brubs's tone was sarcastic. "Seems to me you ought to find another line of work 'fore you wind up on a short rope with a long drop under you."

"Shut up, damn you!" Clanton snapped a hard glare at Brubs. For a second his attention was diverted from Dave.

Willoughby took a deep breath, steeled himself, eared back the hammer of the Colt, yanked it free, whirled and fired in one motion. Clanton's shoulders jerked under the impact of the .45 slug; the Springfield blasted harmlessly into the air, then spun from Clanton's fingers. He toppled from the saddle and hit the ground hard. Willoughby heard the pound of hooves as the horses spooked at the gunfire. Clanton's bay ran toward the fleeing horses, empty stirrups flapping.

Brubs eased his fidgety mustang closer to the body on the trail and stared down at the man called Clanton.

"Is he dead?" Willoughby heard the quaver in his own voice.

"Nope," Brubs said casually. "He's still kickin' some." He slid his .44 rimfire rifle from its scabbard and shot the man in the head. Clanton's body bounced once. The legs and arms twitched, then went still. "Dead now." Brubs levered a fresh cartridge into the Henry. "Never could abide a damn thief," he grumbled. "Man works his butt off to get a little stake together, just ain't fair somebody tryin' to take it away from him." He sheathed the rifle and glanced at Willoughby. "You all right, amigo? You're lookin' a little peaked on me again."

Willoughby lowered the handgun. His fingers still felt cool, but they didn't tremble. "I'm all right. I guess killing people gets easier the longer you do it."

Brubs shrugged. "Depends on who's gettin' killed." A quick grin twitched his handlebar mustache. "Dave, partner, it maybe takes you a spell to pick up on a hint, but you done pretty near right once you got the message. Missed old Clanton's heart by a good five inches, but that ain't bad pistol shootin' for an artillery man."

"Lucky shot," Willoughby said. "Did you ever stop to think what would have happened if I *had* missed? You would have been dead by now."

Brubs's grin widened. "I got faith in you, partner. Besides, I knowed you wasn't goin' to let nothin' happen to me on account of I know the way to Jernigan's ranch and you don't. Now, fetch me my Colt and climb back on that sorry-looking, two-bit plug of a coyote dun. Them horses didn't run far. We'll be in Goliad whoopin' and hollerin' before supper time."

Willoughby retrieved the handguns, puffed the dust from the cylinder of his weapon, and handed over Brubs's Colt. He nodded at the body in the trail. "Shouldn't we bury him?"

Brubs shook his head. "Nah. Coyotes and buzzards gotta eat, too. Reckon old Clanton may give 'em a bellyache, though," he said. "Let's go, amigo. I got a sudden itch to get shut of these jughead horses and jingle a few coins in my pocket." He reined Mouse after the horse herd as Willoughby mounted. "Gonna be nice to be a rich man, partner. And I know these two sisters up in Goliad —"

"Brubs," Willoughby interrupted, "I'm beginning to wonder if there's a woman in Texas you *don't* know. Most likely, both these sisters have large, angry fathers, in which case I will consider this just another one of your ploys to get me killed."

"Dave Willoughby, you are just et up with sour, like you been gnawin' a green persimmon. And after all I done for you, to boot. Ain't it all worked out so far?"

Willoughby moaned aloud. "I must admit it hasn't been dull. Let's trail some horses. I could use a stiff drink right now."

Brubs chuckled aloud. "By God, son, you're gonna make a real, genuine Texan yet."

Bass Jernigan leaned against the porch of the ranch house, worried the stem of a battered pipe, and glared at the two men standing before him.

Jernigan looked more like a common cowhand than a wealthy dealer in horses, Willoughby thought. He was a wizened man with a face the color of worn saddle leather, a jagged scar that ran through heavy stubble from left jawline to earlobe, and one foot toed out at the end of a bum leg. His cotton shirt was frayed at the cuffs and collar, corduroy pants worn shiny inside the knees from long days on horseback, and his hat looked like it might have been reasonably new when the Alamo fell. Wild, gray-streaked brown hair stuck out from under the stained hat and a wiry mustache bristled on his upper lip. His eyes were blue, but so pale it was hard to tell where the whites stopped and the pupils started.

"So Stump Hankins sent you boys, eh?" Jernigan's voice was a deep bass rumble, like the sound of distant thunder.

"Yes, sir," Brubs McCallan said earnestly. "Stump said they weren't but one honest man in the horse buyin' business, and you was him."

Jernigan nodded. "Stump and I have done a lot of business together. Where is the cranky old codger?"

"He's dead, Mr. Jernigan," Brubs said.

Jernigan's gaze went icy, the coldest look Dave had ever seen. "You boys kill him?"

Brubs shook his head emphatically. "No, sir. We was friends of his. Mex bandit gang shot him. Led by a man named Delgado."

Jernigan scratched a fingernail against the stubble of his jaw. "So Delgado finally got Stump, eh? Damn shame. I'd a bet the other way. How did it happen?"

Brubs briefly recounted the story of the fight on Mustang Mesa. Willoughby noticed that Brubs didn't embellish the story too much, which told him something about Brubs's instinctive wariness around Bass Jernigan. "So me and Dave took Stump back home and buried him," Brubs concluded. "Then went to Delgado's place and got our horses back."

Jernigan cocked an eyebrow. "You boys either piss live scorpions or you're just plain dumb lucky if you braced Delgado and got away with it."

"We was lucky, Mr. Jernigan," Brubs admitted.

Jernigan puffed at the pipe in silence for a moment, then grunted. "Shame about old Stump. I'm gonna miss him."

"Us, too," Brubs added quickly. "He taught us all he knowed about mustangin'."

Jernigan lifted a skeptical eyebrow. "I doubt that, McCallan. That'd take at least two whole lifetimes." He shrugged. "Well, let's go take a look at these horses you brought in. Maybe we can make a deal." He limped toward the big corral behind the house where the cavvy waited. In a smaller corral, Brubs's sorrel, the grulla mustang, Dave's black, and Stump's big roan nuzzled a bait of corn in a long trough.

"Stump tell you how I work?"

"Yes, sir," Brubs said, respect obvious in his tone. "No dickerin'. You make an offer, we take it or ride on. Stump said you was a fair man and had the best eye for horseflesh he'd ever seen."

Jernigan stopped beside a stocky, muscular Mexican lounging against a corral post. The Mexican carried almost as many scars as Jernigan himself, Willoughby noted. Neither of them appeared to be the type a man would want to cross. Bass Jernigan gestured to the Mexican. "You boys met Martine Jiminez, my *segundo?*"

Brubs nodded. "He helped us pen the horses."

Jernigan jabbered something to Jiminez in Spanish, then listened intently to the rapid-fire reply. Willoughby managed to pick up a few words, but his grasp of the tongue was still too limited to follow the conversation. Jernigan grunted a reply, propped a worn boot against the lower rail of the corral, and studied the horses inside for a quarter hour before he plucked his pipe from his mouth and rapped the bowl against a post to knock the wad free.

"Martine says there's some decent stock here. Looks to me like he's right. They saddle-broke?"

"Most of 'em," Brubs said. "We didn't top out none of the mares."

"Martine says he recognizes some of the Mexican brands. They come from Delgado's outfit?"

"Yes, sir."

Jernigan plucked a tobacco pouch from a pocket and stuffed a fresh load into the pipe. "Judging from the brands," he said, eyes narrowed as he started into the corral, "some of them have changed hands more times than a two-dollar whore. That doesn't bother me." Jernigan jabbed the pipe stem toward the blaze-faced bay. "Saw that horse a couple times. Belonged to a man name of Jake Clanton. How'd you come by that one?"

Willoughby swallowed, suddenly nervous, and silently prayed that Brubs would know there were times when a lie was better than the truth. Like now.

"Found him out south of the Goliad road," Brubs said. "Still saddled and bridled. They was some blood on the saddle."

Jernigan stared hard at Brubs for a moment. Brubs answered the glare with an innocent grin. Finally, Jernigan sighed. "I reckon you boys are luckier than I thought. Jake Clanton's a bad one. Done a stretch in the pen for holding up a mail coach." He paused to tamp and fire the pipe. "Some say he killed a whole family up on the Brazos. Shot a man, his wife, and two little kids, just for the hell of it. Clanton's got a mess of kinfolk around Goliad. The Clantons are a tight family."

Willoughby felt a sinking sensation in his gut.

Jernigan fired the pipe, closed one eye against the sting of smoke, and squinted at Brubs. "Maybe somebody got a slug into old Jake."

Brubs shrugged. "Could be."

Jernigan pinched out the match flame between thumb and forefinger and tossed it aside. "Good riddance, if that's what happened. If I was to know for a fact Jake got killed and who done it," he said with an eyebrow cocked knowingly, "I'd offer some advice. I'd tell them to walk mighty soft around Goliad. The Clantons are a tough bunch. They got this eye-for-an-eye thing."

Willoughby swallowed and hoped his rattling nerves didn't show. He didn't dare look the horse buyer straight in the eye.

"What did you boys do with Jake's saddle and stuff?"

"Hung it up in a tree a half mile from where the south trail meets the Goliad road," Brubs said calmly. "Didn't seem like it'd be worth the trouble to haul it in. Saddle wasn't worth more'n five dollars, tops."

Willoughby breathed a silent sigh of relief when Jernigan nodded and turned back to study the horses.

"See you boys gathered old *Malhumorado*."

"Who?"

"That coyote dun. He got the name from a Mexican. It means ugly or bad-tempered. I bought and sold that horse twice already. First buyer brought him back. Said the dun was outlawed and he couldn't ride him. Second time he went to a buyer up in the Cimarron — that's the Walking R brand on his hip." Jernigan turned his head and spat. "Fits his name, for sure, but I never forked a coyote dun that wasn't a good horse. You boys ride him any?"

"Sort of halfway," Brubs said. "He's got a bronky streak in him, sure 'nuff. I never did get him rode. Funny thing, though. That damn fool horse bucked my butt off ever' time I forked him, and I'm a better'n fair bronc rider, but he never even humped up with Dave here."

Jernigan cut a quick glance at Willoughby. "Happens sometimes. Never could figure out why." The slightest of grins touched Jernigan's lips. "Maybe he's just a little picky who rides him." He shrugged. "I'll take him. You got forty-four head here. Seventeen-fifty on average for the whole cavvy."

Brubs shuffled a toe in the dirt. "Sounds fair

to me, Mr. Jernigan."

Jernigan pointed his pipe toward the smaller corral. "How about those four?"

"Personal horses," Brubs replied.

"I'll give you a hundred for that roan. Never could trade old Stump out of Choctaw."

Brubs ran a hand across his week-old whiskers and glanced at Willoughby, a question in his brown eyes.

"Mr. Jernigan," Willoughby said, "that's a very generous offer. But I've grown rather attached to that horse. I'd rather not sell Choctaw."

Jernigan nodded. "Reckon a man ought to have one good horse and one good woman in his life, at that," he said. "I had a good horse once. We got a deal?"

Brubs's face seemed to light up. He offered a hand. "You just bought yourself some horses, Mr. Jernigan."

"That suit you, Willoughby?"

"Yes, sir."

Jernigan pushed away from the fence. "Come up to the house, boys. We'll close the deal with a couple shots of good rye whiskey. You want cash, I suppose, instead of a bank draft?"

"Yes, sir," Brubs said. "Where we're goin', there ain't no banks."

The sun was lowering in the western sky when Willoughby and Brubs rode away from Bass Jernigan's ranch. The money belt Jernigan had thrown in sat heavily against Willoughby's belly, its leather pockets laden with silver and bills. Mouse and Choctaw trotted behind on lead ropes. Willoughby's gaze flicked nervously over the countryside as he rode. He became aware of Brubs's stare.

"What's the matter, partner?" Brubs said. "You look like you're gettin' fretty on me again."

"I think I have good and sufficient reason to fret," Willoughby said solemnly. "We are carrying a substantial amount of cash —"

"Don't that just tickle the biscuits plumb out of your oven?"

"And we're in Clanton country," Willoughby said, ignoring the interruption. "It seems to me those are two things that could get a man killed in a hurry."

"Now, amigo," Brubs said confidently, "ain't no reason to go workin' yourself into no conniption. We look like a pair of saddle tramps without a dime between us. Hell, *I* wouldn't rob us. And most likely, don't nobody know about old Jake yet. Ain't nothin' goin' to happen."

"It seems," Willoughby said, his tone cold, "that I have heard that line before."

Brubs chuckled aloud. "We'll get your mind off your frets soon enough. There's a little café in Goliad serves the best steaks you ever put a tooth on, and right next door to the best saloon I ever been in. Then we'll drop in on them Whitehurst sisters. Why, come mornin', you ain't gonna have one single worry in the world, amigo."

249

Willoughby cut a caustic glance at Brubs. "As long as I'm riding with you, Brubs McCallan, I am going to worry."

Brubs ignored the comment. "Just one thing, partner. These two sisters — one's Inez, one's Ina. Inez is the pretty one. She's wearin' my brand tonight."

TWELVE

Brubs McCallan stretched, yawned, and studied the face of the woman beside him amid the jumble of bedclothes.

Ina Whitehurst's pudgy face was bathed in a relaxed and happy smile, her short dark hair sweat-plastered to her cheeks and forehead.

"Well," Brubs muttered, "I don't know how he done it, but he done it to me again."

"Pardon?"

Brubs grinned at the stocky brunette. "Nothin', Ina. Just remindin' myself what a fine time I had here tonight." He patted her on an ample hip, then glanced at the mantel clock on a shelf nearby. It read five minutes until four o'clock. He sighed, rolled out of bed, and knocked on the door of the adjoining room.

"Dave? You done with my woman yet?"

There was a grumble from beyond the door, but Brubs couldn't make out the words.

"Well, you better get done with her right soon," Brubs called. "Her husband'll be home in a few minutes."

"Husband!" The startled yelp was clearly audible through the closed door.

Brubs strode back to the bed and reached for his pants. He hadn't even started on the first leg when the door slammed open and Dave Willoughby stomped into the room, stark naked. "What did you just say?"

"Husband. He's the night deputy. Gets off at four in the mornin'."

Willoughby's face went stark white, then a livid red. "Damn you, Brubs! You never said she was married!"

Brubs shrugged. "Preacher just says words. He don't sew nothin' up so it can't be used."

"Brubs McCallan," Willoughby growled, his fist clenched, "I'm going to pound you to within an inch of your miserable life!"

The Texan calmly pulled on his pants and reached for his shirt. "You might want to put that off a spell. That deputy'll be here in ten, fifteen minutes. He's a right fair hand with that big old ten-bore shotgun he totes around."

Willoughby barked a sharp oath and sprinted for the other room. "Don't forget that there money belt, partner," Brubs called after him. He stamped into his boots, strapped on his gun belt, grabbed his hat, leaned over, and kissed the chubby brunette on the cheek. "Much obliged to you, Ina. I reckon I better go make sure my partner gets all his togethers together before we leave."

Willoughby was yanking on his boots when Brubs wandered into the adjoining room. He tipped his hat to the tall, willowy brunette lounging on the bed. "Mornin', Inez," he said. "You all have a good time?"

Inez flashed a deliciously wicked grin. "It'll do," she said. "Are you fellows coming back soon?"

"Don't you fret that, honey. We'll be back."

"Like hell we will," Willoughby snapped as he fumbled to lace the money belt around his ribs.

Inez's grin faded. "Now look what you done, Dave," Brubs said accusingly, "you done gone and hurt Inez's feelin's."

Willoughby snatched his shirt from a chair beside the bed. "That wasn't what I meant, Brubs, and you know it."

"Don't you pay Dave no mind, Inez. He gets a touch of the vapors sometimes. Plumb excitable, that boy." He sighed. "Don't know what gets into him. We'll be back, honey, and that there's a promise. Well, partner? You comin' along, or you gonna dawdle all day gettin' dressed?"

Willoughby beat Brubs out the back door.

Brubs McCallan lounged against his saddle, studied the swath of stars across the clear night sky, and listened in contentment to the night sounds of the camp on the bank of a small creek forty miles southwest of Goliad.

He worried a piece of bacon rind from between his teeth, took a swig from a pint bottle of good Kentucky bourbon, and glanced at Dave Willoughby. "Partner, you ain't still on the prod at me, are you?"

Willoughby's upper lip curled in a snarl.

"Hell, no. Why should I be? All you've done is bust your butt to try and get me killed in every way known to man ever since I walked into that saloon in San Antonio."

Brubs shook his head in dismay. "I just don't savvy why you got your drawers in a wad. Everything worked out fine, didn't it?"

"Except for being a wanted man with a price on my head, yes. Except for being shot at by bandits, yes. Except for almost being drowned in a river, trampled by wild horses, gutted by a mad Mexican, having thorns and cactus stuck in every part of my anatomy, yes. Except for almost getting killed by an enraged father and a cuckolded husband, and winding up in the middle of a brewing feud with a family of bad men with big guns, yes. I suppose I have absolutely not one care in the whole entire wide world."

Brubs grinned. "Glad to hear it, amigo. I was afraid you might still be in one of them little frets of yours." He took another swig from the bottle, then recorked it and tossed it to Willoughby. "Have a slug of this. It'll smooth out your bedroll and sweeten your dreams."

Willoughby tilted the bottle, took three hefty swallows and came away gasping for breath. He glared at Brubs for a moment, trying his best to stay angry, but finally had to give it up. Brubs McCallan might be a walking disaster waiting to happen, but there was no way a man could stay mad for long at the little banty rooster. And now that he thought on it, maybe Texas wasn't that much more dangerous than Cincinnati. A man could get killed in the city just as easily as out here in the middle of nowhere. *"Tu ne quasieris,"* Willoughby said, *"scire nefas, quem mihi, quem tibi finem diderint."*

"Another one of them philosophers of yours?"

"Horace."

"What's it say in American?"

"It says, 'Do not try to find out — we're forbidden to know — what end the gods have in store for me, or for you.' "

Brubs's brow wrinkled. "Some of them old codgers made sense sometimes, a man studies on it deep enough." The frown gave way to a quick grin. "Why, partner, I reckon them gods has been right good to us."

"How do you figure that?"

"We got us a ranch, a little cash nest egg, a couple of good horses apiece, we had some fine whiskey and finer women, and we ain't lost too much skin doin' it. What more could a man ask?" Brubs reached out a hand. "You ain't gonna drink that whiskey, toss the jug over this way."

Willoughby tossed it back. "So what do we do now? Go out hunting mustangs again?"

Brubs drained the pint bottle and lifted an eyebrow at Willoughby. "I been studyin' on that some. Still got a couple things to work out. We'll figure some on it after we rest us up a day or two at LaQuesta."

Dave Willoughby swished the broom across

the fireplace hearth, a flour sack apron still tied around his waist from doing the dinner dishes.

The carefully gathered ashes swirled away in a gust of breeze as the door swung open.

"Well, if you ain't cuter'n a new kitten on a cozy blue blanket," Brubs McCallan said as he stepped into the room. "You was built outta the right bricks, I'd be flat-out tempted to ask your hand in marriage."

Willoughby shot a hard glance at Brubs. "It wouldn't hurt you to do a little work around here. And I wouldn't marry you in the first place. Wipe your feet."

Brubs slapped his hat over a peg and turned to grin at Willoughby. "Little testy today, partner?"

Willoughby arched his eyebrows. "Who, me? Just because I have to fix the corrals, rehang the cabin door, and do all the cooking and cleaning while you're off drinking whiskey and carousing at Symms's? Now, why should I be testy?"

"Dave, you're soundin' more like a wife all the time." Brubs chuckled. "Don't go givin' yourself a case of the vapors again." He plucked a quart of whiskey from his pocket and put it on the table.

"What's that for?"

"What? Oh. The jug. That's for celebratin' the newest business in LaQuesta, partner. One that's gonna make rich men out of us two saddle tramps." Brubs fetched two coffee mugs from the mantle, strode to the table, and toed out two chairs. "Get that there apron off, Aunt Mary," he said, "and I'll tell you all about it."

Willoughby sighed, untied the flour sack from around his waist, and tossed it over the back of a chair. "What did you do this time? Buy out Symms?"

"Nope. But speakin' of which, Kat's been frettin' about you, amigo." Brubs pulled the cork from the bottle and filled the two mugs. "Poor girl thinks maybe you don't like her no more. How come you ain't been down to see her?"

"I didn't suppose she would have the time, what with you under her feet — or under something else — for the three straight days we've been back in LaQuesta."

Brubs's brow wrinkled. "Why, partner, I didn't know that was eatin' on you. Hell, there's enough of Kat for both of us. I'll even give you first lap at the hog trough the next few days, just to make the biscuits and gravy come out even between us."

Willoughby leaned back and sighed. "It's not that, Brubs. I guess I've just got a touch of restlessness. I think I'll saddle up Choctaw in the morning and take a long ride. Maybe I'll cut some mustang sign. We can't live forever on what we made from Jernigan."

Brubs leaned back in his chair. "Now that," he said solemnly, "brings us straight to what I been thinkin' about."

Willoughby frowned again. "You've been

thinking? That is not a good omen." He lifted the cup, sipped at the cheap whiskey, and winced.

Brubs flashed a big grin. "Partner, you just sit back, take a deep breath, and look around. What we got here's downright perfect."

"For what?"

"I'm gettin' to that. We got us a good, tight cabin, stout horse corrals, and plenty of water and grass in this little valley old Stump give us. You said once you was thinkin' of havin' a place someday." Brubs's face lit up. "Well, amigo — you got it."

"A ranch? Brubs, this place isn't big enough to run more than a handful of cattle or horses."

"It'll run a bunch of 'em for a few days at a time durin' the year."

Willoughby raised an eyebrow. "You mean mustangs?"

Brubs sipped at his whiskey and sighed in contentment. "Here's how I got it studied out, partner. You know for a fact that mustangin's mighty hard work. Man labors and sweats awful hard for a few dollars worth of wild horses."

Willoughby lifted his cup. "Are you riding point on a real trail, Brubs, or are you just circling the herd?"

"By damn, son," Brubs said, his eyes twinkling, "you're catchin' onto this Texas lingo mighty quick. All right, I'll spread this hand straight out. We got a good place here. LaQuesta's smack-dab in the middle of nowhere, plumb forgot by everybody wasn't born here. There ain't a lawman for a hundred miles or more any direction you want to ride. We got us a store, a good supply of whiskey, even a mighty fine whore —"

"Wait a minute!" Willoughby leaned forward. "What's this about lawmen?"

"Think on it, Dave." Growing excitement sparkled in Brubs's eyes. He set his cup down. His hands flitted about, animated, as he talked. "We are sittin' smack in the middle of our own bank, partner — better'n old Jim Bowie's lost gold mine. This here's horse country, and I ain't talkin' mustangs. We done got a market in Texas. Bass Jernigan'll buy anything we bring him. And I'd bet my last bottle it won't be hard to find buyers in Mexico."

Willoughby cocked a wary eyebrow and took in a mouthful of whiskey.

"Dave, we can sell horses top dollar just as fast as we can steal 'em!"

Liquor spewed from Willoughby's mouth as he sat bolt upright. "What did you just say?"

"You ain't listenin', son. I said we can sell horses top dollar both sides of the Rio Grande. And quit wastin' good whiskey."

"Did I hear you say *steal* horses?" The words came out a startled squawk.

Brubs nodded eagerly. "I done figured out it's a damn sight easier to steal 'em than to catch 'em," he said. "And we don't even have to break 'em. No more rope burns or skinned knuckles or gettin' bucked off some bronc in a pile of rocks —"

"You are stark, raving mad, Brubs McCallan," Willoughby interrupted. "Completely and totally insane."

Brubs waved the objection aside as if swatting at a pesky fly and casually topped off Willoughby's mug from the whiskey bottle. "Nothin' to it, partner. We steal 'em in Mexico and sell 'em in Texas, steal 'em in Texas and sell 'em in Mexico. I tell you, it'd be like a river flowin' floodbank full of money, milk and honey. Only, this here river runs both ways."

Willoughby stared in openmouthed disbelief at Brubs. "I can't believe I'm hearing this. *Steal* horses? Brubs, they *hang* people for that!" He shook his head violently. "No way! Deal me out! I am *not* going to be strung up for a horse thief! And that is certainly, completely, positively, adamantly, unconditionally, and utterly the last word!"

Brubs leaned back in his chair and grinned. "By God, partner, we're gonna be the richest men in Texas!" He chuckled aloud. "I already got us a name picked out — what's the matter, amigo? You look plumb near purple in the face."

"Apparently you didn't hear me," Willoughby said emphatically, "I said no. *N-O.* No. Not now, not ever. And not one damn thing you can say is going to change my mind!"

Brubs's grin spread wider. "I knowed you'd see it my way, partner, just as soon as you thunk it through. Now, I know you got this here honest streak in you, and I can't do nothin' much about that 'cept hope you grow out of it. But it ain't like we was gonna steal from honest, hard-workin' folk, Dave. We'll just swipe a few plugs once in a while from some bandit like Delgado or some rich man who don't need the money."

"No." Willoughby lifted his cup and knocked back two quick swallows of whiskey.

"I done got us a name picked out." Brubs topped Willoughby's mug off again. "And I got this picture in my head. A sign. We got to have us a sign so folks'll know we're honest business-men and know where to find us once that name gets knowed across Texas, maybe even several states."

"No," Willoughby said.

"I got some planks, some red paint, some whitewash, and a passel of two-by-fours out there in old Stump's wagon."

"Brubs —"

"We can put that there sign up right smack beside the barn, just as soon as you get her painted. I'd do her myself, but I don't spell too good. I'll tell you how, and you draw it up."

Willoughby shook his head vigorously. "I told you no, Brubs McCallan. I told you no with every negative word in my vocabulary. And this time, I mean it! The answer is no!"

"Now, Dave, you just have a drink there and think on it for a spell. Why, it'd be the slickest deal a man ever seen."

261

"No." Willoughby lifted his cup.

"Now that," Brubs McCallan said, "is one mighty fine piece of work, partner. You got a touch like that feller I heard about who painted the roof of that big old church."

Dave Willoughby swiped a paint-smeared thumb across an itch on his cheek. "I'm not Michelangelo and this isn't the Sistine Chapel. This is a few words painted on some old boards. Someone can use the wood to mark our graves when we get lynched or shot. Whichever."

Brubs stepped back and cocked his head, admiring the new sign between the barn door and corral. The outline of an inverted horseshoe, the brand willed to Brubs and Dave by Stump Hankins, embraced the lettering: TEXAS HORSETRADING CO., and in smaller letters in the center, B. MCCALLAN & D. WILLOUGHBY, PROPS. "By God, partner, we're in business now."

Brubs clapped Willoughby on the shoulder, then peered closer at the sign. "What's this here thing down in one corner?"

"That," Willoughby said wearily, "is a beer bottle. It is my lasting lament over a job I should have finished the first time."